THE NEW-CLASSIC SCIENCE FIC___
OF SHORT STORIES FROM THE LIGHTER SIDE
BOOK FOUR

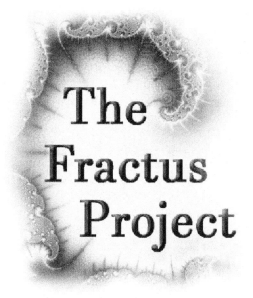

The Fractus Project

TREVOR WATTS

Dedicated to Chris Watts
For her editing skills, commitment and tolerance.

https://www.sci-fi-author.com

First Printing: 2021
Brinsley Publishing Services

ISBN: 9798680555088

CONTENTS

ADDITIVE

'You. Out. You're cast out.' Scuttling into the vat room, that was one way of introducing herself – instant confrontation – proboscis twitching like a fairy's dilly.

'You can't do that. Not to me.' Ha – she stood no chance. I'm already in foul scrooting-up and arguing mode, and it'll only get worse over the next three days. 'I'm in no mood for idiotic jesting by some Ragot in a Red Rok jacket,' I told her plain and straight. 'You really *can't* get rid of me, even if you are the new Over-Manager of the Estate. It's beyond your power and remit.'

So I stared back at her. Waited for her next silliness. I heard we'd got a new Larrad, and I expected she'd come with all mouths blazing, and spewing new rules, though perhaps not quite so soon and so abruptly. 'You want new staff? Get rid of trouble-dregs like me? You *can't* kick me out – I'm a fixture.'

Juggers! The face on her – mandibles at full swell, eye palps abulge with her disbelief, and her rage quotient upped three points. I have that effect on some of the Ragots.

'I've got to stay here,' I insisted. 'You *can't* do it.'

She gave this throat-clearing rattle. It's the Ragots' version of a sneery laugh. Rag-teeth bunch, all of'em. More teeth than chockros, longer throats than Highraffs, and as much humour as a bag of four-point nails.

1

'You can't chuck me out,' I re-informed her. 'I'm bonded to this Estate – fields, vines, barrels, bottles and all. You're stuck with me.'

She lashed out – tempy-temper – but I took a face-slash for it. Hardly the worst thing I've had to put up with since I was sent here, four years ago. The only human on the estate. Scarcely my idea – but they didn't give me any choice at the time – that's the thing about verdicts and sentences. And I been stuck here since. But at least it's warm and sunny and nobody tries to stop me drinking my way into the profits.

'It's y' home now,' they told me – sort of – I had to get it translated. The Ragots have awful accents and juggall understanding of grammar – like they get their sentences upside-down as well as backwards.

So this's home, as they call it. Home – more like a gnome dome – stupid scuttling Ragots live in these round-houses like Zuloid domes, because, apparently, it's tra-jugging-ditional on their home planet which is a totally unpronounceable dump that sounds like sirithiticalyxx Hoym – only you need five times the teeth I've got to say it right, and there's a bass echo from the depths of their throats – they have two throats most of the time, but that varies according to how many mouths are in operation at the time, and what they're using them for.

'You pick now to take the piss?' I snapped at her. 'I'm cast out? As if— Yike!' She was jugging fast with that slash-tip. 'You can't evict me. Where would I go?'

Well, obviously off-planet as fast as I could find a ship with a bribable guard on the tradesmen's entrance.

Juggit, I'm only here cos I got caught – yeah, right – caught by a matic storm when the SS Deliver-in-Time dropped into orbit and I came down on the surface looking for the spares and replacements right when the winds hit the spaceport. I got the units, but some Ragot idiots on the gates wouldn't let me through.

We could have been up and away in half an hour. But no. Not allowed in – too risky. So – bad time of the month then, too, and I shoved'em aside – tried to, anyway.

They're fond of lashing out – and I was too pissed to be re-pissed by them and I lashed back – trouble with that was I was holding a triple-X power rod – very carefully until then – as you would. And I sort of jabbed one of them – poked him kinda over-hard, I suppose. He was feeling foulish and officious, and zapped at me, and his oppo came for me – all glitter-eyes, and tenties in throttle mode. And it was me he was intending to throttle. So I defended myself – still in a temper and a bit of auto-reaction. No – I knew what I was doing, sort of. And thought I could get past'em and aboard with the gear. Except the gates were auto-locked, and the winds were up at sonic rate by then.

So I was taken in. I think they did a kind of prosecution case against me, and I got life. My crew got the units and Ferox blocks, and were out of there faster than a wilko's dick in season. So the Ragots gloated, and they gloat ultra-weird. So there I was, sentenced to life for attacking spaceport officials with ABH intention. Sent out here, the only human prisoner in Hibbith region – on the whole scabby planet for all I knew at the time.

There's others kicking around since. I see them when they visit the estate – we produce a sort of wine that's in top demand in posh resties on three planets. We've developed a unique flavour for the wine, so sometimes we get potential buyers coming round to see what our set-up is. They always ask about the singular taste of our top-seller. 'It's a mix of ingredients that I worked on,' I always say. 'Secret recipe that we perfected. And we work on several settling and fermenting interactions between the ingredients. Yes, the end-product is quite distinctive, isn't it?'

It's becoming rather well-known – the Estate, and the Orina Wine. We're even coming on the tourist circuit now, although Manager Pollo would never dare to allow me to come into contact with any casual visitors.

It's not like I'm a slave here any longer. I have responsibilities now; worked my way up. I know the business – refined the fertiliser balance, the watering and light sequences, lengths, amounts... And there's stages in the fermentation process that I worked on.

I'm not sucking up to them – Jaragoth forbid – simply dragging myself up off the unappreciated floor. I get additional food for the extra hours I put in. And my own room when I got the flavourings ID'd. And I've been working with a couple of Rags, supposedly me under them, but it doesn't run that way in practice.

'Out. You shall be out,' this new Red Rok Ragot yacked at me. 'Now, today. If you have any impedimenta, collect it together.' They don't get the idea of "get your stuff", or just "jugg off". Impedimenta, indeed – paraphernalia... accoutrements. They scarcely speak Yume, but when they do, they go overboard on the big words, and fancy themselves as great wordsmiths.

4

If she kicks me out – A) it's on her head-lobe – I'm here for life, and she hasn't got the authority or power, like I told her. B) where the jugg am I supposed to go? And how? Okay, so I do have a secret cash stash but I dunno if it'll get me through a back-door onto a ship. C). How the pigh-jugging norda is she going to produce such uniquely exquisite-tasting wine if I'm not here to pee in the vat four times a day?

BRACKETS

ERADICATED

CLOSE BRACKETS

'Yoke?' My hearts sank; I knew that voice. I turned. 'I was up in the High Dry Country a couple of days ago. Saw some new immigrant wildlife up there. Looked like it was settling down in a sheltered depression in the trees.'

I laughed at the idea of anything establishing itself up there. So this's Foyd's latest banner news? Anything to get my attention, and a free drink – it's something different every visit with Foyd. 'That's got to be the most inhospitable place to choose. Can't see it lasting long, whatever it is.'

'Maybe they didn't choose.' He looked round for the possibility of a drink.

'What? You think they been dumped? Any sign of how they got there? Driven out of some northern homelands?'

He shruggled his top tentacles in non-caring-ness. 'Who cares where they're from. It's just that I haven't seen the like before, but it's Wildlands, officially; anything's entitled to settle there.'

'Yeah, don't I know it – I'm the Official – remember?'

It was typical Foyd with yet another report; same as every time he came through. So we always grab a bite of snazz and a couple of drinks and we chat, and maybe my mizz joins us with the little ones. The Boys'll join us if they're around.

On balance, it's probably worth me paying for the hospitality every time, while he fills me in about what he's seen and heard from his travelling market floater. It provides me with the gossip from twenty hamlets and villages in and around the high areas for next to no cost or effort. Any major parties trekking through... Somebody new prospecting the peripheral-granite slopes. A cabin being built, or a timber-cutting shed. The Sys Livestock Estate on the East Side was overwhelmed by zaggats – great horde of them attacked at night.'

'Oh Frykit, No. Not the Sys family – lovely people. Torn apart by zaggats?' I have visions of zaggs on bad nights – a mass of ragged glowing teeth and eyes coming howling at me. The bunch we had were in a cage, immediately before we drowned them. But a horde of them, with firebrands and teeth aglow?' I shivered – the succubus of my dreams, the zaggats.

We had the cage on display for a few days, so folk would know what we were up against in the High Country, and not be too squeamish about how we wiped them out. But we had the do-gooders, and the couldn't-care-lessers – 'They can have the mountains; no use to us.'

'Does everything have to be of use?' I asked them. 'The mountains have masses of wildlife, and the zaggats are working their way through it all. We need to follow policy, and release the funding to eradicate them.

They shruggled at me, 'The Coyvers are always felling trees and building dams. The skitters sting anything warm-blooded. The zaggat hunt, roam and kill things. It's in their nature.'

Foyd was trying to earn his drinks, 'Couple of farms over the east side put up lectro fences just after the Sys raid, to discourage the zaggats.

'But I was saying about this new group in the south-east quad – they look different to me – building a big shelter, felling trees, clearing land. They look well-organised. Been there some time, maybe last year? Zaggs haven't overrun them yet.'

There was always something that Foyd had to emphasise, his headline news – it was storm damage last time... huge flocks of Hooyu birds ravaging the pine trees the time before. And this time, it was the new group that was taking over some barren part of the High Dry country. Sounded to me like they were ripe for wipe-out by the zaggs.

Some of his headliners, I check out. Not others. My time's short; so's the fuel allowance. So it's usually worth my while to get the details from Foyd. You don't know what they are, these things up in the High Woody? Numbers? Size? Any damage caused, not counting a few trees?' Not that I cared too much; it's only a small sector of the High Dry, and we get different species migrating through there every year or so, or into there out the way of the lowland farmers – straight into the fangs of the ferocious zaggats that swarm over the whole mountain and plateau area.

'Only saw a few,' he pondered. 'Maybe half a dozen, but there must be more for the amount of land they've cleared of undergrowth. Perhaps they're some sub-type wanting to try growing stuff instead of foraging?'

'Right, can you log in a location? Any pics?' Not that I was all that bothered, but it's as well to log things in. It makes it look as though I'm keeping on top of happenings. And that keeps Central Gov Enviro off my shell.

It was Yes to the location, within a one-hour perimeter – south-west quadrant; nothing of environmental, historical or cultural importance in there. It's equal measures of rock, trees and scrub. No to the pics, he hadn't had the chance. 'Same size range as zaggats. About a third to a half our size.'

'They'll probably get slaughtered by'em before long. Zaggats are nightmare vermin that'll overrun, destroy, slash, burn and kill any rivals. They're my only real concern up in the High Dry Woodlands. They can make fire and shelters; organise themselves; and hunt the other animals. And they'll wipe out anything in their region.

Except it's *my* region. *My* responsibility, as Regional Warden, to keep the vermin under control. That's certified – Zaggats are officially vermin. Numbers to be kept under control. Officially, they are to be "As restricted as possible, brackets Eradicated close brackets".

That's the stated, official policy, "kept under control", which is unattainable. But it's the bit in brackets that gives us a free hand, "Eradicated". Trouble with that is, I'm on my own, officially. My boys help sometimes, but they're on the books as local guides and don't get insurance. So all I can do over the whole vast area is try to keep the zaggs confined within the High Dry.

It's not an excuse – there really is just me, with a small expenses budget. One twenty-year-old scout flier and a meagre fuel allowance. So I don't get chance ever to make any concerted effort on reducing their numbers or spread. I patrol the fringes, respond to any reports of raids in the plantations of livestock farms. And I sure don't have time or inclination to go check out half a dozen newcomers who're going to be zagg-meat within days.

'Next time I'm over that way, I'll check in on them. If I can find any sign of them.'

Bad Year. Lost a tentacle to the zenrot just after that. Mizz and little Trium caught it and so-near died. The Boys left for well-paid jobs down in Cloudytown. Which left me completely on my own for most of the year – me and the older girls, all looking after each other. We did it. We survived. I did my absolute best to keep checks on the Mountains and the plateau – all the High Country. Foyd called in less often. Perhaps he felt guilty at not helping, though I never expected any aid from him. We had a row, too. About how crippling it can be to lose a main tentacle. Accused me of idling away and not backing him up on some access dispute he had beyond the Whitestone River. 'It's nothing to do with me, Foyd. Out of my jurisdiction.' So we rowed about that, too. And putting an over-solicitous tenti round my Mizz when he'd had a few.

He didn't call in much after that, not for a year or so, but other traders and trappers filled me in on bits, like a small logging area didn't look like expanding unreasonably. Three farm attacks by zaggs – another family massacred, and eaten. The other two repulsed the attacks, with around a dozen zaggat dead at each. Unusually high rainfall, some flooding of the High Basin and a few valleys. Nothing different there.

'That new species of something you mentioned?' I asked Foyd next time I saw him.

'No... not seen'em. Not been over there with my market float.' Maybe he was sulking because I was too busy to sit with him while he drank another freebie. He shrugged his top five tentacles in mock sorriness for not having the latest news. 'Been some movement of the Zaggs, though, round there... General movement into that area, it seems like.'

'Oh? You know why?'

He shruggled again. 'Might be ganging up on the new things. There a drink going?'

The following year was better – no catastrophes personally. Family all lived through it. Funds for a new flier. Jake, my oldest, came back with new skills, government paid, and he did a tour of the whole plateau, mostly to impress his new wife and take a vacationary break while showing her the High Dry scenery.

'The Zaggat aren't spread like I remember, Dad. Don't seem to be so many. Yet there's been more excursions of them from the High Dry into the farmlands, where they're getting picked off by better-armed livestock-holders.

Looks almost like something's implementing your Eradication policy for you. Woodcutters were overrun, though.'

'Okay... Did you see anything of those new things Foyd reported?'

'Not a lot, a bit of a settlement, I suppose, a few shelters. We circled round and saw some cleared land up on the plateau, like they're doing some high-altitude farming.'

'I took a load of pics,' his new and very vivacious wife said. 'They don't look like any kind of problem for you; they might be constructing a rock and earth dam. See here on the holos.'

'They don't look anything to bother much about, Dad. Minding their own business. And it's not like *we* can survive long up there, is it? So what they do won't trouble us directly.'

'Indeed not. And, officially, my only responsibility is to control zaggat numbers, preferably by wiping them out.' *And instead, the most my resources allow me to do, is to hope they don't take to coming out the high lands any more than they are doing. I expect the newcomers'll learn the hard way, whenever the zaggs get round to them.*

I was back on almost full form the following years. My tentacle grew back and I felt better than for years. With Jake as official helper, I was able to travel around more, like I had in the first days – what? – thirty-eight years ago.

So, in my travels, I checked on the latest floods, the recent wind-spiral damage, the livestock being introduced higher up the slopes, a die-out of Haargrass on the northern slopes. And, eventually, the area where Foyd had first said the new wilders were building a shelter and felling trees.

I circled the place when I eventually found it, both girls in with me – it was Semiff vacation time, and they were restless to get out the home compound for a bit of fun and tenty-tickling.

We saw several large cleared areas in our flyover, with apparent cultivation, including with irrigation from the dam they'd constructed. Enterprising lot. Tiny figures were moving among the pinacco trees, so I sank slowly down among the trees. They seem so tall and dry and scrubby when they're all around you.

The timber shelter was huge; it looked very settled, almost old. Other, smaller buildings were scattered around. The little creatures were already gathering as I settled carefully in their midst in a wide-open patch of deep forest litter.

We looked out the panas – yes, they seemed to be about the size as the zaggats. 'They're a lot smaller than us, dad.' My girls weren't impressed.

Nor was I. 'Hmm, aren't they just.'

'And thin.'

'They look everso soft.'

'Are we getting out?'

Are we? I suddenly had doubts. But I'd come all this way, largely with looking-in on this lot in mind.

'I bet they don't speak, Dad.'

'They're organised, so they must speak among themselves.'

'We didn't see any zaggat round here, did we, coming in?'

'Do you think they have something to do with that, Dad?'

'Well worth encouraging if they did, Muuse.'

'Maybe we'd best go ask them, hmm?' I unbuckled, let everything whine down, and sidled out the flier, slid to the pine-needle carpet, assailed by the sudden aroma of the pines – the resin smell I'd forgotten.

I gazed around and over the increasing crowd of strange immigrant wildlife. Yikks, there were at least four dozen of the undersized things standing close by, and others further away. I presume they were standing – that's what they call bipeds in an erect posture, isn't it? Only two stabilising and locomotive appendages contacting the ground; two similar appendages that came out the upper part of the mass. Didn't look very flexible. Clothing draped or tight-bound all over them. And a hard-looking lump on the top with an oral organ. Most of them were silent, but a few were making lots of sounds – with that flexi-hole they had.

Trying very hard to relax in the face of such an overwhelming number, I settled, spreading out a little, plaiting my tentacles as relaxedly as I could manage under the circumstances. I waited a moment, and brought a few eyes to the surface and gazed among them. I detected intelligence there… some uncertainty… curiosity. Perhaps a little confidence in their numbers, or their ability. It's not like I was carrying an anti-zaggat flame-thrower, or had anything else pointed at them.

Hmm, yes, I could relate to their attitude; it was exactly how I would have felt in their position. How I did feel, actually. They were wondering what intentions I had, and I wondered the same about them. And what weapons? What else—? No, I didn't wonder any further: their intentions and weapons were about the limit of what I was wary of. Beyond that, I felt relatively at ease in their presence.

Under the shelter, perhaps a hundred slips away, I could see a huge metallic structure. *Was it possibly damaged? A craft from the skies? Could it be possible? They were from the sun? The stars?*

The shelter was unusual – the roof was bobbly. It seemed to be covered in smooth, pale, river stones. *They must weigh as much as a hundred fliers.* I stalked an eye and focused in.

Hmm. Skulls. Zaggat skulls. Hundreds... perhaps thousands. The roof of the whole huge shelter was covered in Zaggat skulls.

Now that is seriously impressive, I had to smile. *Beautiful sight.* I beamed positive thoughts all over the little bipedal beings. *My word – you are good, aren't you? Waging war on them, are you? Or do the zaggs come mindlessly hunting you? Scarce wonder zagg numbers are less than half what they were five years ago. You've got them all here, you diminutive little souls, trophied up on your roof, hmm?*

My girls had slithed out the other side of the flier by then. I wished they hadn't – made us vulnerable. *Why do I feel vulnerable? They're small – not all that numerous; and don't appear to be carrying any kind of weapon. Mind you – anything that can do that to the zaggats... Got to admire'em, eh? All standing there looking at me.*

The girls slid closer to them, eyes peering everywhere among them. Most of them were locomoting away from them, as though nervous – of my two littlies! As if.

The girls were wriggling and tenting among them, so endearing, unthreatening, I suppose.

16

Such numbers – more of them now. All with their oral orifices – and eyes, I presumed – pointing at us. *Fixed-position eyes? Hmm, interesting.* I wondered if a lot of them had been hidden in the sky-craft when Royd first saw them? *Perhaps frozen and thawed as we do with the kiniwakes? Or is their breeding system such that their numbers can multiply from half a dozen to more than a hundred very swiftly?*

I extended a tentacle, slowly, slowly, towards the nearest creature. It made a single locomotive movement away, then stopped. I held my tiptylus there. Sucker-formed the end to a mitron diameter, and held it there in invitation. Beamed my welcoming aura at the still-standing one.

Nothing. Its eye pair was focused on my tiptylus. I upped the intensity; focused more tightly on it. *Come on, strange little creature. Allow me to make contact.*

I sensed its courage as it edged a little closer… I adjusted the height of my tiptylus. It took one small movement forward. I waited and slowly reached forward to its top-mass. It let me make contact. In a flattish area above the eye organs.

We touched. The slightest of tingles.

Gently, gently. No panic here – that would be disastrous. For long, long moments we both held the touch immobile. I let an internal curtain ease aside… permit the creature to glimpse the merest hint of thought within me. *Mustn't let it see all my angst. What are my girls doing over there? Hope my flier's okay. Yeeps – there's a lot of them…*

Come on, come on. Be positive, Yokey. Only positive. Look at that thing under the shelter – it's definitely a sky machine. This's awesome. This whole thing.

So gentle, careful, not scare them off. Don't anger them – I don't want my tentis scorching. Or holes in my buccus.

Opening my cerebrus a fraction wider, not detecting any aggression from it. *Nothing threatening coming to me. Relief was flooding me slowly... Let it see more...*

And I think it's opening a window for me, too. Slow, slow. Trusting, perhaps.

Yes, I'm getting an overall sense of nervous trust from it. More so. Opening to each other a fraction more...

I can discern its thinking. *Although tremblingly fearful of this small mass-zaggat-killer, I detect nothing in its mind that frightens me.*

I focus on the thoughts that it is allowing me to peek into...

'Zyke!' it is thinking. 'I'm sharing minds with an elephant-sized purple and green octopus with a snail shell. And it's having exactly the same thoughts as I am...'

DAINTILY DONE.

Only three more sections to go. Get each one ticked-off:
Approach.

Dock.

Close down.

Get it right and I'll have my licence as Pilot: Space Craft Classes I, II and III.

I'm doing fine so far. Assessor's been giving me feedback on-goingly, 'I prefer to do it that way, Candidate... er, Miz M Daintie.' She's been good that way, probably trying to put me at ease, like, 'and what does the M stand for, Miz Daintie?'

'Millicent.' *Do not call me Millie. Only Uncle Erikk ever calls me Millie.* 'Just the next three actions, then, Assessor.' *Change the subject quick. Don't call me Millie.*

My approach is going fine – she's a sleek little craft, the Starry Jacquie, and I'm accustomed to her. I'm actually good on the manoeuvring, for an amateur – I've worked for Uncle Erikk long enough to pick up the must-do's; quite a few best-not-do-that-if-anyone's-watching's. And lots of the For-Pit's-sake-don't-do-that-ever-again's.

I beeped in to Traffic Control. They confirmed permission to enter. Matching the station's orbit was simple. Under dad's supervision, I've done it lots of times. And a few times on my own – that we don't mention.

Okay, so I have TC's clearance to come in. And I'm easing in and it's a mite tight as well as unlit in the station's entrexit.

Shiff! There's a freighter swinging from its mooring clamps. Three times my size. 'Midweight Class Freighter loose,' I said, for the standard record. 'Side impellors are jetting. He's coming out. See him? He's moving right across my nose.'

Assessor didn't say anything. Up to me. *She's using it as an extra "Response to Emergency" procedure, huh?* White-painted – carrying medic and food supplies; think they own the spaceways. 'You've not got permission to move out. It's me to go in, you, ass-tapper.' Best not say it too loud, or Assessor'll think I got a bad attitude about routine commercial guys.

But he wasn't stopping. No huge deal. He's plenty bigger than me, so that's not an argument I was going to win, so I eased off and held back, hovered outside the white-line zone and watched him approach. Vanguard Shipping – yeah, I seen them around.

Be neighbourly; not cuss the shiffer like I usually would have done. 'Hi, Vanguard.' I beeped across.

No answer.

Again.

So I bipped the alarm. Messaged him. No answer. Again. *Ignorant sod.* Once more, then followed up with the incoming message board. And I put a red ding on it to indicate a One-grade warning that we'd encountered something earlier and he should be aware. To be safe, I extra-detailed it – a magneto burst off Carafja – intensity four and building. He must have received it, cos there was no back-burst signal. Oh, there was – "Foff". Oh. *Ill-mannered schlutt.* So I eased back a little further, minding my tail as I drifted towards one of the passenger terminal docking points: it can be a busy place at the terminal station on Orb. But quiet at the moment – they don't like to expose testees to too much strain, or the regular traffic to excess un-confident nerks raring to cast off their traces.

So this Midweight freighter slips out. Red lights flashing all over the white paintwork. Huh, thinks that giving the emergency alarms is a substitute for traffic control permission, *Shithole.*

Up he comes, all that white hull getting closer and closer. I can't edge back any further and he's going quick for a biggish guy. 'Brace brace.' I buzz to my assessor. She grunts. Corner of my eye, she taps a keypad – Shit. I got a bad mark for something there. Must'a missed something, bastard freighter – Vanguard Shipping. I'll remember him. Hard to forget him, he's hardly a length away, and rolling sideways. He's gonna do a twisting turn and burst. *Toe-rag. Cocky toad in a ship that size.* Not one of the big-big cargo ships – they're confined to the goods-only terminal the other side – but he's as big as they allow in the general movement dock area.

Now there's a passenger liner just lit up his tail end – so he's had permission to move out when clear. And I'm in his way. Delaying a passenger giant is practically an airlocking offence – and my exit is blocked by Mr Ignorant Sod in the red-flashing white Midweight.

Whoa! Whitey's lit up. Tubes aglow in UV, bathing me in it – *dangerous effer.* I tapped the record and report button. That'd go to Control – using Deep-Space power in port! Criminal! Left me in a wobbly wake, though, and I got to shift fast or the Passenger ship'll be reporting me for blockaging.

'Going in,' I announce. Assessor and Control'll pick that up. 'Sorry for delay.'

So I managed to swing her head round, quick jiggle on the thumb drives and Starry Jacquie was nosing towards our designated berth. Feeling the non-existent impatience of the Liner and Assessor and Traffic C, I buzzed the throttle and had her lined-in perfectly. Going in for a perfect docking.

'Change to Berth 8,' comes Assessor.

What!? I can't. Slow up, quick. Fingertouch to TC – 'Permission for B8.'

'Granted.' *Effit. Berth 8? Just gone past it. Slam reversers on? Or slow her to an easy tight circle? Or reverse in. Quickest would be...* 'Brace brace brace. Left turn'. And I had her speed down to 2 star and flipped her over in a barrel turn, really tight – we practise them a lot on the mining rigs when their jetties are swinging round kinda wildly. I was a mite pleased with that. Shuff – shouldn't have done it in confined quarters, though. Too late now. 'Nosing in to Berth 8', I'm confirming with TC. 'Apology for sudden manoeuvre.'

'Kay,' they bipped back. 'No prob.' And we were clicking into place. Auto-grapplers extending from ship to dock, and dock to ship. Extra secure.

There. Done. No. Not yet – Close-down routine – power levels... re-settings, batteries... Lights, shielding, temperatures, passengers double check. We didn't have any of course but it's part of the "Absolute Routine" in case of stowaways or somebody you forgot about. Ah, yes – applies to Assessor, too. Then cargo? Not carrying any. Just a couple of tools crates in the back I need to do a visual on, and clamp-pressure check – yes, all fine. Anything else? Have I forgotten something? Damn-damn.

Announcement to passengers, 'Welcome to Orb Terminal. De-boarding will commence... Mind the step into the airlock...' Anything else? Recontact TC to confirm arrival and docking complete. Sit back. Unstrap.

Now for the verdict. I tried to smile, but it was even weaker than you're supposed to do. 'Don't smile like you usually do, Millie. It looks cocky. Go blank – neutral. Like you're not trying to pressure'em. Not worried. Simply waiting.' So said Uncle Erikk, anyway. And he's usually right.

'Let's move into the back compartment, shall we, Miz Daintie?' says Assessor.

Eff – that sounds ominous. Effit I failed... shi, shi, shi.

So we move to the cargo seats in the back. 'Now then. Let's go over the last three sections, shall we? Beginning with Approach, hmm?' A stern look. *Oh shuggs.* 'Initial approach... yes, fine, Pass... Observation? Pass... Situational Awareness... Pass.'

This was going well. *Yes, but there was that asshole in the white Vanguard freighter.* 'Maintaining full control at all times... Pass. Correct use of communications to others... hmm. Best not to send "Hi". Stick with "Greets", it's more neutral. But "Hi" is acceptable. Pass.'

Next... Docking. Yes. Hmm, control and awareness? Pass. Compliance with regulations including speed... well... and consideration to other users...' *Shuggs – that tight turn? Blocking the passenger vessel off? Giving way to that Red-lit-up effer in White? Not confirming his receipt of warning messages? Oh shuggs – I've failed because of him. Yeah, and everything else.* 'Yes... Pass...

Response to emergency need to change course or speed?' *That'll be him... and the liner... and my little twist into Berth 8... shi, shi, shi...*

23

'Pass…'

'Huh? Pass? You sure?'

Assessor didn't look up. 'And finally, Close-down. Now then… Procedures followed in sequence? There, I'm afraid, is the sticking point, Candidate Daintie. Strictly speaking, you should inform TC verbally of your arrival, before the passengers. So, I'm afraid…' She tailed off. 'That's a grey mark.'

Shi, shi… I usually tell'em before and after, and I don't often carry passengers – never, actually, not legally. And anyway, TC knows I'm in when the sensors register my presence, and by the clamps clicking on. *Shuckit.* Totally pied-off about that. *Effit. I effing failed.*

'Okay, yes, I understand that,' I said. 'Thank you, Assessor. Next time, hmm?' I reached to shake her hand in thanks and courtesy.

'There won't be a next time, Candidate. Not after that performance.' I got the frozen stare then. 'We're not finished here. Firstly, you should be more pleased than I detect.'

'I failed. What's to look—'

'You certainly have not. What? One grey mark? When you haven't even got anyone in the passenger compartment? Doesn't count. Grey ones don't count anyway – non-safety items. No no – that was as clear a pass as I've ever encountered. I might hope to see you piloting yachts, passenger launches and ferries… mining rigs and midweights, in the near future? I may perhaps see you again when you go for your Up-weight licences, hmm? *Pilot* Daintie?'

Effit! I passed! Passed! Passed! Wait till I tell Uncle Erikk.

24

'And then there's the matter of the Midweight white Vanguard pilot who ignored TC, exited his berth without permission...' She referred to her note-tab. 'Lack of auditory warning. Use of emergency-only lighting, dangerous manoeuvring in confined space, making use of ion UV power within the docking area. Total disregard of the speed restrictions and safety concerns of other users...'

She took a deep breath and continued. 'Failing to acknowledge standard communications from other craft; failure to acknowledge warning communications.'

Another pause for breath and a glance at her notes. 'Heading directly towards a potentially life-threatening region... in this case...' she consulted the pad again, 'a Magneto 4 anomaly, which is developing into a force 5 as we speak.'

'Yes, I shall report him. So many offences. If he survives the Mag Storm, I can't imagine him being allowed behind the console of any craft for a long, long time.

'Congratulations again, *Pilot* Daintie.' Assessor closed up her note-tab and looked around. 'Now – I'll get on with sorting out Big White Van man.'

FAME

'Hello. What's this, then?' Eyes riveted on the screen, Morris's hands felt to both sides, one reaching for the keyboard to let the world know, just in case this really was *a Discovery*. Well, he conceded, perhaps not *everyone* in the world, just three dozen fellow astronomers who would be awake and observing the heavens at this time. His other hand was automatically confirming that the recording apparatus was running, to make sure he would have proof of his discovery.

He watched, checked the calibrations and focus, the azimuth settings, the recording levels and the parabolic waves that only a few hundred other people worldwide understood with regard to the 12-inch telescope, especially when pointed within the solar system, instead of looking for a sight of the gravitic waves up Andromeda's spiral arm.

Morris Morrison was supremely patient in his work methods, and equally desperate for an advancement in his position, for fame, for recognition as being something more than a 'scopic pudding. Ridicule, though, would be worse than his present anonymity. 'Yes,' he studied the object, 'it's definitely new to the solar system. Doesn't fit the trajectory of any known object. Unlikely direction, too. Almost looping in, over the plane of the system, and then curving in across the ecliptic, as though gravity-pulled. But it's not quite right for gravity influences... have to check it out through the data recordings.'

He studied a mass of binary data for the object carefully, and did a swift on-going analysis. *Must make certain of its trajectory and nature,* he thought. *Its basic characteristics, before leaping to the alerts. But... but... suppose it is totally new? And someone else puts out the first alert and claims the glory?*

Increasingly hopeful, he considered wider, *What if this object is something new, and totally different, not simply yet another dwarf planet, dark comet or Oort Cloud object?*

It just didn't fit. *Perhaps it's of a completely different composition to other celestial bodies?* He could feel his heart rate rise; his lips suddenly becoming drier. Could this be *it?* His fingers were aching and twisting to press the auto-phone link on the keyboard and assure his instant fame – relatively speaking. One press would pre-empt all others that followed. It would register him as *the spotter* of a new celestial body within the solar system – a *something different* body. And it would inform all other watchers and informees of its presence, along with all his available data on trajectory, mass, speed, plotted direction for origin and destination.

This could be it. My moment. But of glory? Or ridicule? Damn damn damn... a little longer, make sure. Check again... and again. What other factors and considerations were there? Think. Think. Is this my moment? I can claim its discovery. Check again, and again... a little more. A little longer. Be very sure. Who else would be studying this region, this focus, tonight? He could think of at least a dozen others who did so regularly, and the skies were clear over most of the relevant places tonight.

Perhaps not as clear as here, on the peak of Mauna Kea, Hawaii. But plenty clear enough if the scopes were pointed in the right direction.

Ah, at last. A visual image, so minute. Little more than a dot. Another. Come on – three to make a trackable sequence. Ah, yes... there, I have you. Another. You do exist. And I can prove it now, with black dots on a white screen, as well as printouts and four hundred kilos of binary data.

His fingers hovered. He'd never released an alert before. Or, actually, yes, he had. Twice. But both times a fraction too late – seconds. His alerts were still winging in the wifi ether whilst others had registered before him. Such crushing disappointment.

Kāne! What the kāne is it doing now? The tiny body's trajectory was changing again. Wow. Impossible. Unless some huge dark object with a powerful gravitic influence is particularly close to it, unseen, and affecting its course.

His desperate finger pressed the key. *There. Done. I shall have the priority over any other keys pressed on the system worldwide. Mine the credit or the derision.* His heart sank in fear and thumped in hope.

Seven minutes, he mumbled. Seven minutes to be spread over the network, checked that no-one else had registered the object in the last few moments. It would be confirmed or denied by any system that was awake and operating and could swivel to check. Then, one way or another, it would be Morris's object.

Two thirds of the world's great telescopes would be in daylight now; and most others would be engaged in surveys that could not be changed in their scheduling. But they would all receive the information, be theirs to check.

If there's been no other claims yet... he hardly dared to breathe... he couldn't walk the ten feet to the work surface where his flask and sandwiches stood, already, like Morris, part-consumed.

Kāne! This is so exciting. Come on. Come on. My astronomical heritage awaits, he melodrama'd to himself, as a colleague had once taken the mick.

Nothing for long minutes. He turned back to the screens. It had gone.

Instant panic, then despair when he couldn't relocate the object. *Where? where? Ah. How the kāne did you get there?* The echo was faint, and he struggled again to get a visual image, something more than a data-set.

Ping! A ping! It's registered. *To me! It's mine! Whatever it is. But again... Where is it? Finished? Broken up? Changed trajectory impossibly abruptly? Must be a different one. No... it's the same one. Identical mass.*

Back-tracking was impossible, considering all the radical changes of direction it had undergone. But now... *the data's changing – has it broken up? Split in two? Or spun? If it was disc-shaped, its apparent size would vary in a spin.*

The pings came in. Other scopes had begun to track the object, along the Pacific rim from the Rockies to Japan, New Zealand to here in Hawaii – the McClennan VLT, just 200 yards away had re-programmed to follow this object. *Oh, God, I pray it is something. They'll never forgive me if it's a false reading.* Others were logging on as phones rang and the news spread. Logging on; three observatories coordinating in a joint loop-up.

Oh God. My first, and it's breaking up already. The shortest-living... Before we even got clear visuals on its shape. But I got the marker shots – eleven in sequence, all told. With precise time-links to the mass of binary data. There's no arguing with that.

Come on... one good, clear visual to define its shape... Impossible! It's reforming. The fragments have re-solidified. God, yes... I'm getting pics – two, anyway. That'll do for CNN and the New York Times. In fact, he studied deeper and closer, *It's coalesced tighter than before. Denser. Must be...* he checked and rechecked the calculations... almost three kilometres diameter at the—

'Impossible.' Blipped Hijo Kaido on the Mt Sakamura VL. 'You fix. Is joke.' Hijo the Doubter, Morris always thought of him. He sneered at everyone else's discoveries. Who cared? He's never registered anything.

Yeah, well, I care. My reputation isn't going for a Burton. Er, my potential reputation. Morris Morrison was hyped up over every possible nuance of the whole situation. It had reformed. Or rotated onto its side? And not changed direction for several minutes.

'What the fack ya doing, Cobber' Oh, hello, the Anglo-Aussie Array is up and running, huh? Wally the finger-happy wombat was probably jealous he hadn't created another fake alert himself.

'I'm getting this the same. This is real, then?' China Doll had come online.

'Yes, it's real.' *Oh, God... I've done it. I've got another hour at most of usable darkness. I got the first pics. The others'll have bigger and better as this thing comes closer, but I have the first. The first ever.* Little more than a dot. Then a diffuse mass. Like a blurred spark.

Even re-pixeled, expanded and spectro-enhanced, it wasn't much better.

As it took its fourth change of direction, he drafted a swift press release-cum-colleague-alert with the first pictures attached, along with a speculation and statement of its unique behaviour, its seeming independence of gravity, as though alive and swooping, apparently changing shape. Like a shoal of fish or a murmuration of starlings, he tapped out to the unsuspecting world. No time for more – the others would be key-jabbing their reports – he stabbed the final key to publish, and be damned by world astronomical opinion.

There. That's it. Morris sat back. Daylight was upon him, and he would be unavailable for some time. He only had the one night booked on the Mauna Kea Scope, videoing the whole night so that he could assemble a series of illustrative shorts for The Astro Society back home. All about how the 120-inch worked… its wonderful size and the facility as a whole… 'That's it,' he sighed. 'I've had my paid-for time, and twenty-seven hours solid awake. I need to sleep – no choice now. Night,' he muttered to the room, as he finished packing everything away.

Morris Morrison slept for twelve hours. Several other sites tracked the astral body, each confirming a similar erratic trajectory and variable density/mass estimates.

Speculation was already mounting in the astronomical world – and spreading to the general population as several news channels latched on, but were then starved of information as the body had swept past the Earth and was currently thought to be somewhere between us and the sun

– and, at that size and unpredictability of movement, it had been lost in the daylight glare.

But, eighteen of the world's major telescopes changed their schedules and recalibrated their azimuths, coordinates, projections and shift patterns, amid intense cursing about lost and paid-for projects. The others either didn't dare to upset their sponsors by dropping current work, or their telescopes weren't the right sort to focus on anything closer than five astronomical units away. So they stayed aloof and pretended not to be jealous, and tried to not show excess interest.

Morris's brief missive to the ether was 98% regarded with derision, as the clear implication that it was a living thing was read into his 27-word statement.

"The shoal", the papers called it.

"The swarm", the TV channels said, and paraded his name with ridicule.

"Morris Morrison's Mob", the New York Times sneered, with a picture of Photo-shopped starlings swooping round the moon.

"Morrison's Murmuration," snooted the Times.

"Mo-Mo's Swarm", derided the Daily People, complete with hopelessly inept Photo-shopped images comparing Morris' face with a swarm of bees, under the heading, "The Things from Outer Space".

Virtually every media outlet in the world had it on their Wacky Silly-Season page. A few took it more seriously, and wondered aloud, in a variety of "how daft a conspiracy can we make up?" stratagems.

It was gone and Morris was disappointed, as well as practically in hiding. His access to the vast telescope was gone – that had been his solitary session with it. He was due on a flight home to Gatwick in a fortnight. 'I mean, I don't get to Hawaii every year', so I'm staying here for a much-needed holiday-cum-hideaway. It works out very cheap, seeing as the flights are paid-for already.'

Although scoffed at on the TV, newspapers and Net, the astro community was more measured. Its public pronouncements varied from, "No comment" to, "We're looking into it" Private reactions ranged from, "What the fuck possessed you to cancel everything to watch some bloody ghost image?' to, "There is definitely something there – these data streams are absolutely genuine, and inexplicable in any other way. Keep on it.'

But it had vanished. Morris kept checking his connections in the astro world. Several dozen of them were convinced that something had been there, and they worked on the pooled data that Morris had begun to gather. They had added to it and reshared it multi-fold. "There was definitely *something*", was the consensus.

Ten times a day, he checked – seeing his fame not exactly how he'd craved it to be, but it was there – he wouldn't be forgotten, "Morris' Missing Monster" was the least of them. But he tried to find diversion in the volcanoes of Halema'uma'u and Pu'u'o'o... and the lava tubes and high black cliffs... the rain forest and the waterfalls... the markets and beaches... the sunbathing and flesh ogling... the surfing and snorkelling.

'But none of it measures up to the excitement of that night in the observatory,' he self-commiserated over his third or fourth Paniolo Pale with a Spit-roasted Pineapple Gin chaser in Laverne's Sports Bar.

It was on the six o'clock news magazine – an interest item on BigIslandTV. 'Remember Mad Morris's Cosmic Swarm? It looks as though it's been seen again—' He was upright, shocked, amazed, yes-yes-yessing to himself, and all ears. It had been observed again. Much closer now, and still in a changing, swinging trajectory. There were pictures... speculations.

Someone changed channels. 'This's a sports bar, stupid,' they said, and re-tuned for some silly game of rounders... baseball, whatever these Nancy fools called it... But yes yes yes! It's back... closer...

Morris looked around, triumphant, 'I do like Hawaii,' he and his drinks agreed, and ordered a bucket of mahi mahi and chips with tomato ketchup. 'Perverts – no vinegar,' he complained.

So... a few more self-congratulatory drinks later, he wandered back to his condo half a mile down the road southward out of Kailua-Kona, and checked on the laptop. 'Yes!!! It's there! Big... the Russian OST happened to be facing vaguely in that direction, and had taken nine good-quality pictures in a close sequence before the object suddenly semi-dissipated and veered away – its shape altering drastically in a few moments.

"The Comet Conundrum", the Honolulu Gazette put it.

All night he sat up, half of it slumped on the keyboard asleep, but checking across the multiple sites that were picking it up now, including hundreds of amateurs with 6" to the occasional 50" telescope. The data was amassing, complete with pictures and theories. '*My* object,' he kept murmuring in modest, private, self-delight. 'I'm famous.'

Within moon orbit it came now, so much closer than where it had been at the time of Morris' initial recording beyond the astcroid belt. And it was curving in tightly towards the Earth.

Its imminent arrival was anticipated in a mix of total disinterest, up to religious fervour fit to rival Madame Pele. 'It must be living,' proclaimed the devotees.

Size estimates varied from a few kilometres' diameter to almost a hundred k, and not just because of observers' mismatches – it really did expand and shrink, stretch and reform. "It's either a sub-ethereal spirit being, or could it really be Mad Mo-Mo's swarms or shoals?" World opinion was being guided towards the latter.

'I'm getting really famous now,' Morris marvelled, a touch afraid that his fame could rebound on him if the object did turn out to be alive. 'God! I'd have a god named after me.'

As the mass swooped into a series of elliptical orbits around the Earth, becoming closer on each pass, so the details became clearer. It was a mass of individual parts. And they split apart, spread, re-gathered, changed direction. 'It behaves exactly like a shoal of herring, or a flock of murmurating starlings,' said Director of Naturology Adiwidya Goblok of the Indonesian Institute of Nature.

'That's what I said,' Morris declared in Laverne's that night.

'That's what Morris Morrison said five days ago, with far less evidence,' The interviewer noted. 'Something of a genius, don't you think?'

Adiwidya Goblok huffed and puffed and talked himself out of a job.

Morris said no more, but his five-day-old photograph was on every channel, and he was lauded in Laverne's as the representative of Kapihe on Earth, he who prophesised to King Kamehameha that, "The ancient kapu will be overthrown and the altars of the mighty will be cast down and the hosts of the heavens shall come down and eat them all."

They were taking it seriously, too. Many native Hawaiians were totally believing in Mo'Mo, the living foot-servant of Kapihe. The rest just went along with it, wondering if they ought to believe, to be on the safe side.

Morris didn't have to buy another drink – and wasn't asked any probing questions – for Kapihe would speak through him when he was ready. He passed out around three in the morning, very happy, apart from wondering what would happen if his prophesy was true, and the swarm came down to Earth and ate everything.

But he wasn't capable of verbalising his fear by then.

Time and darkness being what it is on Earth, along with observatories' inability to see in the light, news might have been patchy, but there are satellites that see close-up objects very well indeed, and the pictures came flooding in. 'These things are gleaming black monsters... they are presently shaped like torpedoes or fish, but they seem to have scales that may be opercula that hide something beneath. Wings, perhaps, for if they enter the atmosphere. Or fins, legs, weapons, mouths should they come to the ground? Who knows?'

'Size?' Was the most-asked question, closely followed by, 'Why is it here?'

The swarm seemed to have settled around thirty thousand kilometres above the Earth – between the orbits of the Galileo and Glonass satellites. But not for long, as though making up its hive mind, its swarm mentality.

The point of decision had seemingly come.

The descending swarm – a closely-estimated and agreed total of approximately two hundred million

37

individuals – dropped from orbit in an inward-spiralling curve, and landed en masse across the islands of south-east Asia, a mere four thousand miles from Laverne's Sports Bar. Early cell-phone footage, much live-streamed online, showed creatures the size of ocean supertankers. And they were ravenous. They ravaged the land and people and trees and crops and creatures that crept and crawled and vainly hid. They scoured and scuttled like vast battleships. They fought each other, dismembered each other, and devoured the land in two hundred million coach-sized mouthfuls per minute.

Mo'Mo's Plague, it was coined as, until the irony of it occurred to someone, and it became Moses' 11th plague. And the swarm creatures became known as Mo'Mos.

'Oh, God, I'm famous,' and he sought refuge in Paniolo Pale Ale again.

En masse, the creatures jostled and jumped and hopped and devoured northwards and westwards through Thailand and Myanmar to Bangladesh and India, finding lush forests and fields. They left a desolation of featureless scoured land, devoid of any signs of life except a few hundred of their own dying, part-dismembered remains as the swarm repeatedly leap-frogged itself westwards.

'The Arabian Desert will stop them,' was the confident cry from the Director of Natural History at Nairobi ER Institute, Dr Chepkirui Mwangi, approximately one hour before the first of them landed, over-filling the grounds of the Institute, and began to eat everything within range of its appendages, mouths, orifices, and kilometre-long claws. Director Mwangi promptly went the way of Director Goblok to Mo'Mo hell.

Progress across Africa was inexorable. 'Definitely MoMo's 11th plague,' it was agreed. Fame had indeed come to the good astronomer.

On Hawaii, it was largely a matter of distant, removed interest. Apart from the fabulous demi-god Morris Morrison, of course, in his personification of Mo'Mo, foot-servant of Kapihe, messenger to King Kamehameha. He still hadn't bought a drink or a meal – the supremely welcome guest at Laverne's Sports and Gods Bar in Kailua-Kona, who brought in more custom than Obama had done.

The swarm devastated Africa, leaving mashed and lifeless landscapes of uniform brown rock and dust behind, littered with the obligatory thousands of dead, dying, and dismembered Mo'Mos.

'That'll be the end of them,' predicted the supremely confident Director of the National Institute of Natural Sciences at Manaus, Brazil, Professor Antonio Silva. 'The Atlantic Ocean is wider than the Arabian Gulf.'

He was about as wrong as anyone could be, including Directors Goblok and Mwangi. Following the Emptying of Africa, as it became known, there was a one-day pause while the creatures congregated and fought and bickered and eventually launched themselves, as though they could smell the lush forests of South America in the winds.

'You'll never get a flight off Hawaii now,' Morris was told at Kona Airport. 'All flights are cancelled, whether west to Japan or east to the mainland. Fear of landing in a newly-infested area is stopping everything. Go back to Laverne's – they need you.'

It took the Mo'Mos a week to work their way up through South America, and across to the Pacific coast... swarming and clambering over each other along the isthmus of Central America towards Mexico and the United States. There, they faltered and fought on the verges of the barren desert lands.

As the next stop on the Mo'Mos' food conveyor, Hawaii held its collective breath. Leilani Kahananui, Director of the Hawaii Institute of Island Environments said nothing and crossed her fingers.

Morris Morrison, inebriated but accustomed to it by now, saw the coverage on the television in Laverne's. And he studied the progress of the enormous mass of two-hundred-million-and-counting creatures that had circumnavigated the globe, and come at last to the final jumping-off point before they descended on the Hawaiian Islands.

'They number at least triple that now,' according to someone in Oxford who could count and knew these things. 'Well over half a billion.'

'It strikes me,' Morris said to the beer-buying customers in Laverne's, 'that Hawaii is safe. That the Great Wrath will not visit us. The forecast of Kapihe is coming true. We are safe. We are the chosen people. The kapu are gone.'

It was several weeks since he'd first spoken in there and been recognised as the messenger of the Gods – a kindred soul with Tūtū Pele. Thus, his words now, though slightly slurred, were clung to by all. The wonderful news spread from Laverne's God and Goddess Bar around the world in seconds, via cellphones, with live coverage of

Morris making his intoxicated but sage-sounding pronouncement.

News of his God-sent intervention and rescue spread around the islands more slowly, from bar to bar, home to home. But by dawn, everyone was breathing again, and knew for certain that they had been saved by Kapihe's god-companion who resided at Laverne's Pele and Mo'Mo's Bar in Kailua-Kona. "Hawaii is safe from the ma'i ahulau o nā mōneka – the plague of monsters. Mo'Mo has made it so."

Around noon the following day, Morris Morrison, companion of the greatest Hawaiian Gods, Pele and Kapihe, together with Laka, Kihawahine, and Haumea, awoke clear-headed to the news that the great horde had gone from the Earth, banished by Mo'Mo. It had launched itself skyward to mass trepidation and wailing in Hawaii. But its flight had continued upwards, and it had left the planet altogether. After circling in two increasing-height orbits, it was presently heading towards the sun.

To either side of Morris, as he made his way from his apartment to Laverne's, the crowd split apart, many falling to their knees, or casting lei and orchid blooms at his feet.

The first steps of The Great God Aumakua – protector of all families, appearing among them in his new Earthly form of Mo'Mo – were beamed live around the world; and throughout the islands to an utterly rapturous and worshipful horde of around one and a half million Hawaiians.

No-one asked *how* he had prevented the Eternal Death from descending among them. No-one would ever dream of asking the Gods to explain their methods. Suffice that he had saved them and the islands.

Yes, he thought, as he approached Laverne's, I remember seeing some David Attenborough programme on the telly, with all these millions of locusts that swarmed in huge masses just the same. Right at the end, when they'd all eaten up, laid new ones, split their shells, or whatever they do, they all started chittering and climbing on top of each other and doing little launches into the air. A load more fussing than on previous departures. This signalled that they were preparing to depart on their ultimate flight, never to be seen again. David said so.

These space creatures were doing something very much like that last night. They were readying themselves for their final departure, not merely another quick hop to another feeding place.

Besides, Hawaii's so small it'd only be a ten-minute snack. Not worth their effort.

And, besides again, if I'd got it wrong, what did I have to lose?

FOOTPRINTS

'So real, living dinosaurs walked here? On this surface?' I looked at the three impressions in the flat rock part of the beach, 'and a dinosaur actually made those footprints?'

'Yes,' he said. 'Stand in one of those, and you'd have been trodden on by a huge long-necked dinosaur – but it was 165 million years ago. This rock was soft mud back then, when the British Isles were in the tropics – drifting north with tectonic movements, you know?'

Yes, I knew that land masses moved, very slowly, 'We had tropical-jungle-type countryside around here?'

'Exactly, scorching hot sun, humid, real rainforest climate. The whole landscape's been dried out and hardened and buried for millions of years since then.'

'So, the sea wasn't there?'

'It was probably somewhere in that direction, further out, and this was all mud banks with sluggish rivers drifting towards it. Most likely tidal – flooded every day.' He waved around, behind us, 'And the cliffs weren't there at all – it'd be all very flat, sub-tropical forest then, with palms and ginkgoes and fronded plants. There're beds of twiggy and leafy fossils in the rock beds over there.' Student-Steve knew it all, like quoting his professor's lectures. 'Monkey puzzles, too – the really high spiky ones. You get fossil roots and branches all the time. I found some in a rock bed higher up the beach a couple of days ago.'

'It's a wonder they came this close to all the amusements... and the crowds on the beaches in Whitby and Scarborough.' My girlfriend, Erica, has funny ideas sometimes, and doesn't listen much.

'It was millions of years before people were around,' Bright-eyed Steve was very patient with the unlearned, 'And it'd be baking hot, a tropical jungle,' he repeated for Erica's sake. 'This was a muddy riverside, a delta or estuary like the Mississippi or Ganges. In India, you know?' No, she didn't know. But Erica had other fine attributes, without troubling the intellect.

We carried on chatting. He knew everything about dinosaurs and their footprints, but I knew more about Derbyshire fossils than he did, cos there were lots of leaves and bark and branches fossils in the seams of coal in the village where I grew up. I was saying that I used to go collecting the fossils in the spoil heaps, and dig them out of the exposed rocks. 'I always imagined the ancient forest all round me, all dark and hot and great big centipedes. All them trees dying and rotting away made the coal layers, you know.' It was my turn to quote somebody who taught me – at night school.

Yes, Stevie did know, he'd read about them, studied the ones in the university's displays.

'Ah, but I used to collect the fossils out the rocks,' I told him, sort of triumphalistically, 'and draw pictures of what it must have been like back then, and I Googled the environments. I stared into them and pretended I was transported back then and the forest was all round me. I used to dream about those coal forests and mighty trees and ferns and giant mares' tails. I imagined I could smell the rotting wood and leaves… and feel the sweltering heat and hear the chirruping of insects.

'"It's unhealthy in a 12-year-old," my mum used to tell me. "You're obsessed."

'"Interested," I'd tell her. But she was right: I couldn't stop thinking about them, and I have a terrific collection of

44

fronds and patterned bark impressions and even a pine cone and some fossils of roots called stigmaria. They're even older than the ones from around here; mine are about two hundred million years older.'

We must have been nattering for an hour or more, and walking round, and he showed us some other depressions that he said were dinosaur footprints, preserved in the rock. He cleaned them up and carefully drew round them with a stick of charcoal. And I was getting the idea much more – 'Is that one? And these here?' And I was right.

'You've got your eye in,' he said. 'It usually takes people ages to get the idea of what they're looking for – the three toes, usually; the angles between them, the heel digging in…' He drew round them, and I smudged the charcoal with some wet seaweed, so the markings weren't so unnatural-looking.

'Hey, that looks much better than my crude lines,' he said. 'Must remember, and do it like that in future. You should look on these other beaches.' He drew a crude map in his notebook and tore the page out for me. 'You'll find some good ones there if you've got your eye in for what to look for. And it looks like you have.'

He said he would have offered to show us, but he was joining a study group for a couple of days, on a field trip in the area. They were staying in Whitby, and he'd try to join us in the Duke of York that evening – 'But we're students, and you know what that means when we get in a gang on the town.'

He didn't turn up, but we were fine on our own in one of the little table-booths, with fish and chips – well, you've got to in Whitby, haven't you? And I was telling Erica how I was really made up with this whole idea of dinosaurs being round here, trampling through jungly forests and over steaming mud-banks. 'I can't imagine why, but it had never occurred to me that such things as fossil footprints existed.'

Erica still couldn't imagine it. But she was very imaginative in other ways, and that more than made up for her disinterest in fossils, especially when we'd sunk a few drinks, wandered along the pier and watched the waves bursting along the base of Tate Cliff.

'You know,' I tried telling her, 'I used to ride my bike – and eventually drive – into the Peak District, and I used to collect different fossils, from under the sea – they're preserved in the limestone rocks. I used to look round quarries and in the walls round fields, and read all about the different sorts of corals and shells, and sea urchins turned to solid rock.'

'Hush, Freddie...' she kept squeezing my hand and slipping a hand inside my shirt. To be honest, I was actually torn about it – I was still so upped about the fossils – even the coral reef ones I used to find – and I'd visualise being under the water, strong sunlight on the waves above me... the water warm all around... fish... great banks of corals... oozy sea bed with crawling things and shells. I absolutely used to live in those places – round the coral reefs, and in the tropical forests. And now I was starting to do the same with muddy deltas and herds of migrating dinosaurs that—'

'Freddie, do concentrate,' Erica was insisting. And she can be very persistent in her persuasion. But she did have a lot to offer; and she was definitely offering it tonight.

So I put away my childish thoughts of books on fossils and geology, of web sites and night school sessions, and turned to matters of men.

Mmm, yes, Erica certainly had one up on my trays, cabinets and catalogues of fossils. If not two up, actually. On the other hand, I thought later, if I could find and collect a fossil of a dinosaur footprint... For myself. My fossil collection.

My dreams that night! So vivid. I was seeing dinosaurs, tramping sedately across those steaming mudflats, some small and chasing each other. A giant predator – a Megalosaurus. With a mouth the size of a fridge, full of teeth like steak knives. Stalking the long-necks – but I was among them, and it had its eyes on me. I was feeling its breath.

No two ways about it, I had to explore at least one of the beaches that Stevie-the-Student had told us about. And if the art shop was open, I could get some charcoal and a brush to show up any footprints I found even better. They'd look good on the photos.

Erica wasn't too keen on that idea – the lure of the shops, and all that. So I went alone. Tiny pull-in that I squeezed the Focus estate into, finding the overgrown footpath along the clifftop, and down a steep section where there was a rope to help. Fishermen put them there, but don't make them public knowledge.

It wasn't a broad bay, maybe two hundred yards from one rocky headland to the other, and between them, the beach was a rock platform with scattered patches of sand and shingle, boulders and seaweed. Sure enough, a fisherman was on the rocks of the far headland, dedicatedly gazing out to sea. Nothing would take his attention away from whatever fish he was casting for – cod, probably, plus whatever else happened by.

But I was there to find footprints – dinosaur footprints created 165 million years ago... so long buried... and recently exposed again as the layers of rocks that buried them had finally been eroded away. What amazing luck to happen upon such things before they, in their turn would be worn away to nothingness.

I stood there, on the sand, staring at the bare, near-flat shale bed right in front of me. 'I don't believe it; I've found some footprints myself. After only five minutes down here.'

They really were – dinosaur footprints pressed down into what had once been mud, and now solid rock. I walked round them – a group of depressions covering an area fifteen or twenty feet across. I so nearly got down on my hands and knees to kiss them – talk about ecstatic.

Three different shapes and sizes – the two biggest were rounded, a foot across, with a crenelated edge at what I assumed was the front – like a row of toes. This would be one of the long-necks, huge and heavy... something like diplodocus that ate leaves. And three, maybe four the same shape, but smaller and not pressed in so deep. Must have been a youngster long-neck. Mother and child, I thought. Wow – how great that must have been. If only I could have been here, seen them walking across the mud, towards the next slowly meandering stream...

And the third set of prints was completely different – three long, thin toes spreading out in a triangle – like a bird's. Big bird – must have been ostrich-sized. A theropod – hunter – predator. The ones with teeth and claws – like those in Jurassic Park. Awesome! It must have been stalking this pair, or maybe even a whole herd of long-necks, looking to pick off a small one, like wolves hunting deer or bison.

I cleaned them up, brushing the sand away, exposing two more impressions. One was a double – the hunter treading through the large rounded one – So it must have been following them, stalking them, if the mud was still soft enough to take the foot, then it must have been around the same time.

I shaded them in with the charcoal, quite delicately, tastefully, I thought, and they looked incredible. Like new – like coming to life. I sat on a boulder when I'd finished taking photographs and doing sketches of the site and measuring each print. And how far apart they were. The drawing I made would look great in the display cabinet I was suddenly designing in my head, specifically for dinosaurs

I had to sit and open the bottle of flavoured water, crunching an apple – the finest that Morrison's could sell. It was just too much – like when I'd collected coral fossils and imagined swimming through the warm water – me and Steve Irwin.

What a revelation this weekend was proving to be! I couldn't get over it – Dinosaurs had walked over these great stretches of what used to be mud! And by sheer chance, their footprints one day back then hadn't been washed away by the next tide or overflowing river. And here they were – as if waiting for me. What a gorgeous fantastic day this is. Warming sun, dripping and Marmite sandwiches to look forward to for lunch, and this – my best fossiling day ever. Completely mind-opening.

In a dream exploring the other rock platforms, finding two more groups of footprints – both the hunting therapods, different sizes. A row of four and the other was just two of them, not really clear, only about six inches long, with great long raptor toes for slashing and gripping. Maybe the same height as me, like birds with very nasty attitudes.

Joy-of-effing-joys! I found two little footprints on a fallen slab – each three inches long. Perfect size to slide into my rucksack. I've collected my first dinosaur footprint fossil. I kept repeating it. Planning exactly where it would fit among my collections – right on the fireplace in pride of place – at least for a time while I built the display cabinet specially for footprints.

It must have been a baking hot time to dry it all out solid before the next river overflow spread fine mud on top of them all, and buried them – until now, when all the later rock has been washed away by wind and tides.

This place was magical – a whole new world. I was living that day as it had happened, so long ago – A single day preserved in time. Just effing awesome.

Someone else had struggled around the other headland, a small party of students with a tutor. From the logos on their hi-vis jackets and hats, I imagined they were checking a shale bed for oil content – with a view to off-shore drilling sometime in the future. They concentrated on a layer of rocks just beyond their reach up the cliff. I had to smile at their struggles, and tried to spot my younger friend Stevie among them. Couldn't tell, and they never turned their attention away from those rocky beds with their potentially oily mudstones and shale beds.

So all was peaceful for me with my array of wonderful footprint impressions, and I puzzled over some tiny

depressions scattered across the surface. Strange –
Raindrops! That's what they are. From a brief shower
that day. Preserved ever since. It came to me that it was
so real, as if I was right there, in Jurassic time. Running
fingertips over them, 'It's impossible. Ridiculous that a
trace of something so tiny could remain – in the middle of
a tidal estuary.' So hot and humid, so much nearer the
equator than Whitby is now. I gazed around and could see
it all in my mind.

Not the cliffs of nowadays – but the vast palm trees,
the monkey puzzles and ginkgoes… the mares' tails fifty
feet high… ferns crowding round the fringes, invading
the mudflats.

What huge creatures roamed across these flats then?
Could there be the giant Megalosaurus, as well as the
smaller ones whose footprints I had found? Hunting their
prey, the foragers between the forest and the waterways.
Is that how that day was, so long ago? Muggy and humid,
with a shower that pock-marked the surface, and
dinosaurs trampled their feet over the same mud, stalking
or avoiding each other?

Looking round now, at the barren sand and rock, and the
cliffs at the top of the beach with their layers of mudstones
and shales slowly being eroded away. How much it had
changed. Everything, actually.

Except… these raindrops. And, over there, a curved
line of shell impressions and plant remains on the rock
surface – just where the highest swish of a wave had
come at high tide. To pinpoint a moment in time like that!
I was amazed that the utter normality of a single moment

could be preserved – effectively for ever. And *there...* some stones sticking up from the rock surface – just beach pebbles. But there was a swirl pattern around them – where the last wave had swept over them, and receded, leaving skirt-like rivulets in the muddy sand – still there.

If I half-close my eyes, I can imagine the ginkgo trees over there, the huge cycads and pine trees crowding tall and close, hiding... who knows what? The mud squelching and sucking under my feet. The smell of rotting vegetation arising. A riper stench as I almost stumble over a clump of seaweed. No, it's dino dung. Yeuk – it's soft and fresh.

In my mind, the cliffs fade beyond the tops of the encroaching forest. That's not the fisherman's dogs chasing each other... they're iliosuchus, or some such small dinosaurs, hunting tiny prey. The mud stretches way off. It's not a group of students with their tutors over there, towards the sea: it's a family of long-necked cetiosaurs, being stalked by a pair of megalosaurus. Hope they don't look this way, I laugh.

My rucksack's feeling heavy. Maybe it's time for lunch and a drink, reduce the weight a bit. The sea seems so blue. I'm sure it wasn't forecast to be anything like this hot today. So humid, too.

So recent, these footprints look, as if they were only just made. In fact, they look as though they're still soft. And these have splattered my own booted footprints from an hour ago. That means... I looked around, behind me, 'It *can't* be.'

I stilled, absolutely. Sudden afraid. A head peering from the edge of the forest. The same size as a horse's head. A mouth opened, but that was twice the length a horse's could ever be, and no horse ever had teeth the like of these.

I watched – maybe I was spellbound – fascinated with the realism of my dream... my deepening imagination. The way that thing took almost hesitant steps, as though testing each one before taking it. Looking everywhere in advance of each movement. Somehow, I felt compelled to remain as unmoving as possible.

It was heading after the small group of long-necks that were lumbering along the water's edge towards a clump of palm trees, crossing the trail where I had wandered earlier. Long-legged; slow, cautious movements, each foot in turn poised for a moment before it was laid carefully back on the soft ground.

The sun so much hotter. I was breathing better, felt livelier, despite being rooted to the spot; energised. A buzz. a dragonfly the size of a model aeroplane zipped closer across the mudflats, coming straight at me. I took a step sideways, ducked.

'Shit.' The thing, the stalker, had stopped and turned towards my movement. It was focused on me. *Thirty or forty yards away, is it?* So still I kept. Knowing it had seen me.

Damn. Don't be so ridiculous. I straightened up, knowing I could shake my head and it would vanish.

Still it was there, closer. Despite shaking my head again, rubbing my eyes. This is impossible. So hot, so damp, humid. I'm sweating, exposed in an area of tidal mudflats. It has, it's definitely seen me. It's taken a couple more steps in this direction. Fixed on me so intently.

This is so stupid. It can't possibly—

GAMZE AND THE MODRIGELL
VISIT CENTRAL CITY

'I truly would never have visited Central City if I'd known.'

'It's your own fault, Jerry. You shouldn't have won the Hortus Gardeners All-comers prize for the largest Modrigell on record.' There were times when Joycabelle reminded me about things, quite unnecessarily. 'You should have read all the rules and conditions before you entered.' Sympathy and empathy aren't in her vocabulary banks.

The sand in the cream was just that the prize-giving ceremony was to be held in Central City this year, at the HH Hall. My fellow villagers in Brynn's Lea very much insisted that I attend in person, when they found out.

'You *must* go.'

'We *got* to see you on the TriVee.'

'It'll make Brynn's Lea famous, planet-wide.'

They only found out because Joycabelle bragged about my win in the Toggler' Oop she attends. And *she* blames *me* for the trip to Central City. Huh.

Yep – so with all the pressure, we had to go, me driving our big old kosho wagon with the kids lined up along the back seat in age order from the left – Alphy, Betty, Gamze, Deltoi and Epiphy. And my huge prize-winning Modrigell fruit almost filling the back bed where I usually carried the barrows, mini-plough and cutters.

'It looks like Gamze,' Alphy unkindly said. Actually, that was true enough, but I tweaked his nasal protrusion to teach him not to be hurtful to his sister.

We started off along the local roads that I'm accustomed to, and it was great. Everybody had banners out, all congratulations and well-wishing. That's a gardener's joke; well-wishing means they're hoping you fall down a well and drown. They're a bit of a funny lot in the village, but they mean well; or is *that* a double pun on something?

I pulled onto Highway 6, the south star road, for only the second time in my life. Last time hadn't been wonderful. That was when I collected my limp – a broken leg sustained when we collided with another vehicle. It was only the third accident ever on H6. Joycabelle's still the only person on Hortus who still thinks it was entirely my own fault. 'You must have mesmerised the other driver into steering straight at you, Jerry. I know what you're like.' Not that it had anything to do with her sitting next to me with her non-stop yapping sufficient to drive me to suicide, of course.

It was fine this time, though I was a nervy-knot by the time we saw the city spires looming out the distant haze. But, still in one piece and undamaged, we arrived at the overnight hotel on the city outskirts in the late afternoon. The HighSide was directly off the Highway, with its own slipway; easy to find and access, especially with the AutoDrive that had cost me a pretty pengő to have fitted. I'd booked the place solely for that reason – least trauma for me. Serendipitously, it was a marvellous super-tech-style place that the kids were delighted with. That made five out the seven of us.

The bratsquad, loved only by me, Joycy and God, explored the attractions within the place for a couple of hours. Then I unlocked the suite doors and let them back in. Joycabelle and I had succeeded in our first three *really* High-Rise Bonks ever. And super-high-tech the facilities for that were, too. If we'd come back home straight after, it would have been plenty memorable enough for me. But the outcome of previous such spectacularities was performing a mass clamouring at the doors. So we had to desist from further such frivolities of a carnal nature.

I should have known better – filled with the joys of the newly-discovered high-T hotel, they insisted I accompany them to the spire-top viewing floor. Little pervs – they knew I'd be ill up there. I went, but I really wished I hadn't – I'm a gardener, not a city-admirer. All it did was make me even more nervous about the day to come – Central City's spires and globes were all lit up in the midnight blackness.

'You really expect me to take the Mad Pack in there, Joycabelle? Among all that mass of spikes and spires?'

'Magfuckingnificent,' my youngest declared, just before she developed a bruised audiflap.

'We should all be in bed,' I told them, nearly widdling myself at the thought of our impending journey into the midst of *that* lot.

Went to bed, but couldn't sleep. The kids didn't go to bed, but slept for the first hour of the city-bound journey in the morning.

**

It was like an All-kid Auto-Alarm went off when we entered the city limits. They all woke up at once. Bright, alert, and full of Wows, Zoops and Yarroohs. 'Dad, we got

57

to go up *there!'* pointing at a Skyway Ring Road that curved through the sky.

'No way on Hortus,' I told them in a no-uncertain tone.

But I did. Not of my own volition. It was the auto-C part of the highway. Central had taken us over. Some algorithm somewhere had total control of the kosho. And whooshed us up a near-vertical rampway in a *really* throat-sickening heave, and we were up in the high levels of Central City.

'We're in midfuckingair!' Deltoi declared, clearly begging for a fattened lip. 'Dad! Dad... Dad...' all the time.

'Look at this...
'that...
    'those...
'up there, down there...
        'over there...
'between them two needle spires.
        'Daddaddad. Them towers are twisting.'

They were – two needle towers reflecting brilliant silvers and golds of the sun on glass and metal. And they were slowly rotating. Yeepers to the Zoogs and back! They were something else. Don't have stuff like that in Brynn's Lea.

'We got the corders on 360-full-go to show all y' friends when we return.'

'If,' I said. 'If we get back.' Not that I could ever face peeking at them.

"The azure river sinuously curls through the city like a gigantic writhing snake, cut by smooth-arched bridges..." Ye Zoogs! The city blurb was as vomit-inducing as the sky-high twists and turns, even without the in-situ views that hurtled and whooshed from here to Bedregone. The bridges even had people walking or triking across them.

We zoomed under one at three-G.

Hovercars on curving rails that tangled themselves in knots and entwining junctions. A glass tunnel with power trains that hurtled off like a bullet in a glass barrel. C-City had them all, and put us through them all, every single mind-bending one. Utter torture that the five-strong Death Squad loved. I reckon they programmed my navvy to do the full tourist tour on Automatic.

Neat-laid parks alongside the river… garden patches and assembly areas… mighty statues and obelisks. Shidders! This place had them all, and threw them all at us in spadros.

We came to a click halt in a glass tube, like a one-car station with exit platforms. Sagging in relief, I reached for the latch.

'No, Dad, we progged it for an extra.' And that was Betty – turned traitor on me.

"Thrill of your life." The neon flashed, sickeningly, just as the cab trembled – like something taking hold of us. And up we rose like a screwing rocket – literally screwing a spiral into the sky. Totally independent of rails.

'It's the… Tractor… beams…' the dead-when-I-get'em-home pack gasped their delight.

Joycy was practically on the floor with me. Blaming me, like for the way she brought them up to be defiant little monsters. All I was doing was gulping and gripping as we twisted up and spun over. Fruggerty! We were right above the whole city! Poised. Hung there. And I just knew… We were going to drop and we'd all be terrified – I would, anyway.

Sure enough. A vertical fall – power-accelerated into a twisting barrel roll and a loop between two spires, and we glided to the smoothest of stops beside an alightment platform – carpeted in azure and white – like clouds. It was the hotel. Yes, yes, I confess – I had made the booking myself, for the kids' sake. Thought they'd like it.

Didn't think what the actual room would be like – I mean, the foyer reception was normal enough with pseudo-desk and those waify things that hover all round making whispery little sounds… I seen'em on the vids. Creepy, they are.

And our room! It was the top of the needle. The whole floor. Circular apartment. 'The Owner happens to be a garden-lover – realised you'd won some garden… plant… flower competition world-wide – and thought it would be nice to let you have his personal apartment – there's only the Sky Garden above it. No – you won't meet him – I believe he's in orbit round New Orcan or some such seaworld.' So said the flunkey in blue and white, looking a right platt.

It was sickening. Dizzying views in every direction. The kids ran round the panorama windows for the first hour while I went up the Sky Garden and loved the creepers – vines and staff. But they didn't have Modrigells as big as mine – or balls, by the look of'em.

So we had a meal in the main restaurant – all red and gold and not-so-subtle lights, but the music was okoi and the food was out of this world, 'Well yes, it was this morning, Sir. Just imported from Poller on the daily arrival.' Thus spoke the waiter who scarcely ceased his bowing routine till he nearly spilled something.

'With such a limited time here, Sirs and Ladies,' his fellow server was a creep, too, 'you might consider taking a NeverDrop pill, and don't bother sleeping. There are walking tours – just log on at the desk – or I can do it for you – and the moving pavements will glide you anywhere – fixed routes, most popular sights, sky-tours.'

'Dark, quiet, underground tunnels?' I suggested

His lip sneered on its own, and the Mad Pack overwhelmed me, anyway, 'Dad we got to…' and they were all over the pervy waiter and gave him a huge tip for the idea and the bookings – three separate trips! I was destined for a death of ten thousand high-city horrors.

Evening and all night! Standing on these moving panels that slotted into roads, and they knew where you'd booked for and you could ask for a table and chairs and call for a meal and it was delivered by a fluckerting drone while all these mile-high lit-up buildings slid past and glowed and had tiny cars and trains looping round them – I was smab-gocked. Even the kids shut up for a minin – while they were stuffing food down and trying to get my drink.

'Fluckit,' I said and ordered'em their own sixty percent proof drinks. 'Hoped it might knock'em out,' I said to Joycy. No chance, not with the NeverDrop pills inside'em.

So some time around mid-morning the following day, we found ourselves at the HH Hall, where the committee

61

was waiting for us – and the other category winners, of course. Treated us like royalty from Reum, they did.

We had a grand presentation, interview on World Vid – with side pics of everybody in Brynn's Lea cheering us on and we waved to'em and it was so exciting and fabulous. The kids said that, not me.

We had more meals and drinks and talks and laughs with the other winners and hangers-on and groupies – I didn't know gardeners had fan clubs. I have. Now. Gamze and Betty run it. Gamze was a favourite. 'How'd you manage to grow a kid that looks like a Modrigell?' And all that joshing – so of course, she was deliberately putting a couple of leaves behind her ears to enhance the effect.

So. That went on till about midnight and somebody programmed us to return to the hotel and we were all still high as hovercars till we found the waiter with the NeverDrop pills and got the antidote – the Sleepies.

The over-hyped five were nodding in moments – bliss!

Come mid-morning, time to be heading home to Brynn's Lea and we loaded the still-dozing kids onto the back seat. I got somebody to programme us directly home, no messing and no diversions.

We must have been well onto Highway 6 when they eventually woke up – like after fifteen hours kip.

They were straight into being full of it again. 'Dad! Dad! That was fabulous.' I could see the worship in their eyes – I got a good imagination. 'You going to win again next year?'

I'd been thinking about that. Mostly, I'd been thinking of throwing the seeds and fertiliser away and never looking a Modrigell in the eye again. But this morning, when we bade the hotel staff farewell, I looked out for our waiter friend, 'You got any more of them Sleepies?'

He had – a wholesale pack-full. They're on the back tray where the giant Modrigell was. So, armed with them…

'Well,' I said to the eager back row pack, 'Can't guarantee winning, but I'll have a go, eh?'

GIVING THEM A HAND.

I gave them a hand. Or not exactly gave it to them. But they've got it. And they're keeping it.

There were three of them – huge Rangat males – coming after me right out the blue. They ambushed me out by Calinger's Feralair farm where I'd been repairing some machinery. I was keeping an eye out for them, because Charlie had been killed just down the track only a few wekkies ago. Very nasty way to go – ripped to shreds and eaten by Rangats.

Shoiks! I don't know how I got away so fast. I'd left the buzzy-bike in gear with motor on idle, and it shot off within a half-second. That was a surprise, they usually stall or cough on a leaping start, especially at dawn on a planet as cold as Mimador III.

I absolutely hurtled round the Four-Cap and across Big Plat fields. It's all of two mills from there to here, under the blue-tone lights, at that.

But I kept the speed on max, even on the turns, which is Big Risk Two, after Rangat Males at Big Risk One. Didn't breathe all the way down, just going, 'Come on come on come on,' and geeing the buzzy with my knees and fists and backside. Nearly lost it to a side-skid round Ethan's Bends, but I was staying just ahead of them – triple mass of slash talons and razine teeth in my wake.

Nearly there at the marshalling yard. Hurtling hard-over through the main gates into the open turning area.

The roll-up doors on the storage gate started lifting when I was fifty away, and these three Rangats were barely a length behind me, doing eighty. I buttoned for the roller-door to start dropping again and figured I'd just about make it ahead of them. Not too soon or they'd get in there with me, and that'd be fatal for all of us. And not too late, or I'd be stuck out here with them. I wouldn't stand a chance, not even against one.

So – down the door started coming. *Fraction too fast, too early!*

Racing straight at it. But. No. I had it about right – *Yes yes yes!*

Dropping the buzzy onto its side at full speed, I went skidding forward across the yard. I'd make it – scuffing and burning on the 'crete, but I'd make it.

I was half under the door, zapping through with not even a brad to spare.

Yoik! What?! My arm was stuck. I spun. Must have been a ground fixing bolt that caught my sleeve. My arm behind me. My hand was the other side of the roller-door as it crunched down the last fraction. Dead flat to the ground, and then slotting flush into the groove.

That brought me to a dead halt. It had me trapped by my skin, and probably sinew as well. Not bone – I'd felt all that shatter apart.

Yesss, the blood was pouring out, pumping away. I was in total shock. Couldn't believe it. But I knew it had happened. Not a dream. It was true and happening. My hand was the other side; *they'll have ripped it to shreds by now.*

Needed to get my arm free – get at the stump. Bind it up. Stop the bleeding. Get the Triple-X before the pain starts.

Dammit. I'm in deep-deep dung now. This'll be my third body-part replacement. I'm only allowed three. Then I become the bank for the others.

When I was found guilty, I wondered why the sentence was so short.

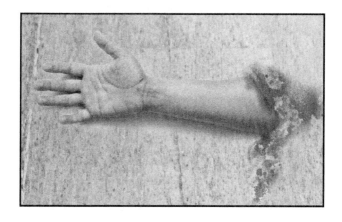

GUILTY

'Yes, it was in a courtroom on Zedex. Yes, that's the one – planet with two huge moons, practically a triple-planet system. You don't know it? Okay, I'll tell you what occurred last time I was there. You getting the drinks in first then, Dubium?'

Yes, he was.

'Don't worry,' I told him. 'It's worth the price of a pijiu.'

It took him under a minin to get the three drinks – which is pretty good going in a red-and-neon scrapyard like the Armpit of Armageddon, with the crowd they get in there. 'Zedex was one of these places they ran like their own little fief, regardless of United S&S policies and conditions.'

'Bit of a pirate hole, I heard,' Skepty was recalling.

'You got it,' I told him. 'US&S was getting a tad unchuffed with'em, some of the things they did and thought they'd get away with.'

'Oh? Such as?'

'Confiscating cargoes... Cancelling legitimate contracts... Accusing crews of smuggling... Occasional disappearances... of passengers, goods, even ships.'

'They can't be doing that!' Dubium dismissed the whole idea. 'Central'd be after'em.'

'No. Not in the Realm. Anyway, I was there, only passing through with my supplies for the Exo-globe Observatory – mostly low-tech tools, foodstuffs, medications. Mainly for their Immigration and Customs requirements.

'I was bringing my ship down to the surface in Zedex Terminal Main. It was a port for mixed lower-sized ships – cargo, passengers, local of any kind. Located right alongside the long-distance Passenger and Ferry Hub. Both busy places, all in all. Maybe a dozen craft of all sizes coming and going in the Main and the Hub at any single moment. Don't have too many bumps, though, with their tractor-beam network to keep things apart – Magno-beams lock on us when we call in and register.

'I was heading down – locked in with the Magno beams, and I saw three of the home-based glitter craft harassing a visiting mining ship.'

'Glitters? Fast little craft? Very manoeuvrable?' Skepty knew something about them.

'They're the ones. Locals use them for all their general trading, cartage and carriage. Run by irresponsible dealers and bandits. Think they're gods... run the place like they own it. Like with this Rikel Ore Carrier they were picking on – stun-shots, in the way, blanking the communications and the Magnos – really dangerous stuff. Port Authority was completely ignoring it – looked like a common occurrence – their idea of fun.

'Sure, I was watching. Not interfering, especially when I was in process of landing on my designated pad. The space is cramped in there; unlit surface; awkward tightness for a craft like mine that's more like a latticework than a regular hull-shell ship. The Lady Vindicta was mostly cable and piping, with the various cargo containers clamped and cabled on – they're all enveloped in the field when we power up.

'So I'm being extra-careful guiding the Lady in, keeping one eye on these idiots, and this guy gives me the bow-buzz as I'm going in. Suddenly over the wifi these three're telling me to mind my own business. I haven't done or said anything, just kept a V-rad on them. They don't speak Standard – ignorant shurters – but they made it clear enough I gotta keep out their way. Like that's possible when I'm going down on a Magnolec beam dead straight to my allocated spot. Rearwards, of course, in the Lady Vindicta. And there's no stopping a nine-tenths-finished landing sequence.'

'Yes, there is.' Dubium sipped his drink, contradicting me, at the risk of getting the next round in as well. 'You do the Pause and Delay.'

'Not in a senile bag of yonks-old military surplus vessel like the Lady. Once you set it into sequence, it's not going to stop for anything. That old girl used to drop attack troops into active zones, and there was no provision for manual override – not when attacking. Once you're committed, you're in. Dropping them or collecting them – you don't stop for anything. It assumes you're under fire, or risk of it. And it acts accordingly. Perfectly okay, normally.

'So I get this armole of a glitter-bug zipping right under me in my Magno track and there's nothing I can do when I'm in auto-land. So he gives me a slash underneath. Bloody disruptor bolt, right across my landing carriage gear. I can't do anything about it, and he's still dodging round down there and gives me another. Crippled my landing e-quip.'

Duby and Skep nodding and imagining it – they'd been in enough busy ports to know the setup.

'Retaliation is automatic – it's built-in on an ex-military craft. No changing that. Can't dig into the works of a Space Force ship, even a second-user one like the Lady Vindicta.'

'So? What happened?' They were all ears, open mouths and thermo-gasps. They're funny like that, the Litors – all agog at the thought of a military confrontation in a civvy cargo port.

'You didn't retaliate? Fire on them?'

'Not me. Lady V did. Took out all three. Single Zee-bolt each.'

'You vapped'em?' Skepty was finding this delicious.

'To microns.'

'You didn't get shot up?'

'You got arrested?'

'By the Zeds?' Duby was head-shaking in wonder.

'Yep.' I finished my drink and looked at it significantly, but they didn't rise to it. 'Found guilty of causing unjustified death, and sentenced to termination – execution. "Guilty", the judgement was. They told me that on the way in. "You caused twelve deaths – absolutely unwarranted – and massive destruction of their ships." They were going on about them being local on-planet craft – all legit and minding their own business. Penalty was automatic.

'I'm telling them that the first one was firing on me, and my auto-system took him out – then their two fellow swipers came at me with magno bolts, and I was still in settlement sequence; "So my retal guns auto-ed in, naturally. And they only got one mode when under fire. It's called Total D."

'Right up there in their courthouse—'

'Courthouse?'

'Mmm. Zedex Judiciary. It's their Law-and-Order HQ. Where it all happens.'

'Their Legal Node?'

'That's what I just said. But they act like pirates. It's government-sponsored and raked-off.

'I was telling them they really shouldn't execute me. "It ain't right," I said. "I did nothing wrong. It's their own fault for assuming I was going to interfere in their piracy. I wasn't – I don't approve, but – what the hekl – local matter – somebody's going to be monitoring it all, I'm thinking – no problem. I got my own difficulties, schedules, priorities…" Would they listen? Would they chuff.'

'So there I am, incarcerated in some State-run pirate court with all their wiggies and tentackers – obviously a daily routine for'em. Set some newcomer up – execute him – confiscate the ship and the cargo.'

'I expect they didn't think they'd lose three craft doing it, though?' Skep finished his drink.

'I don't suppose they did. So that made it more serious than the usual bumps and crumps, I imagine, and I'm dragged off. "Special session", they said, though it looked as if they held two a day.

"You are guilty as charged. There is no defence". Says the left-hand judge in the gold braid fake.

'"Sentence will be carried out at once," comes the one with silver epaulettes.

'"You have one minin to make your peace – contact relatives, or employers, whoever. Stay calm in your space." They said it like it was routine for'em. My Space? Yeah, right – cage, more like.

'"Okay," I told'em, like I'm nearly in tears. 'I'll contact my HQ base. They're aware of the situation."'

'Yeah?'

'And?' Duby was all ears – almost literally. Litors are like that, too.

'I dabbed through to Base on my Tee-way, and I told'em. "Okay, gimme the lift outa here in five, huh? Yes, I put self-detonation in place. It'll take out the whole of this place, when I explode. Yes, thank you, bring me back to my own body in three, two, one—"'

HIGH SPACE DRIFTER

'Commander, M'am? That rogue craft coming in from above the ecliptic?'

'The High Space unidentified vessel?'

'Yes, M'am. It's approaching Must-Action Distance.' Sub-Cap Bard looked at me as if I was going to give him an order immediately. *Like what? Blow it to the Vac and Back with a novatronic bomb?*

'And it's still heading directly for Fortex Base at Vrenh?' I said, and went over to look at the screens and the streams of data that flooded them with updates every few seconds.

'Except we're in its way.' Bard looked at the other officers around the control room to make sure they understand our position.

'That's why we're on forward station – to guard against incursions by enemy forces.' *Okay… things are becoming a little tense, but this shouldn't be a huge problem: we're the ASN Annihilate, a destroyer class Warship, around three times the estimated size of the incomer. With enough firepower to wipe out a swarm of almost anything, especially a small, Terrath vessel. But it was still at extreme range for visuals or detailed data collection. Best be ready.* 'Weapons to orange status,' I ordered. 'All systems to Standby.'

**

My Sub-Cap called out again, 'Mander? We have a first visual.' The screen largely confirmed what we had deduced already.

'It's a drifter,' EN Raigh chipped in. 'No motive power detected. Possibly crippled.'

'It's barrelling end over end,' Bard added after a moment's study.

I clipped directly into the analysis stream myself, absorbing the sparse and uncertain data that our out-monitors were collecting. 'Mmm,' I agreed after a time. 'She's cartwheeling. Send preliminary notification to Base: "Un-ID spacecraft incoming. Apparently not under control."'

We watched the flickering speck on the screen as the craft tumbled towards us.

So this is to be my opening action as the first female commander of a capital ship in the ISN? There had been no response to our challenge, so our next step would normally be to destroy it.

But a ship barrelling in like that? Nothing normal about that. 'We're on our own, SC. We'll have to make the decision. Maintain full alert.'

'It's definitely a Terrath vessel,' The SL Officer called across. 'T-12 class. Not capable of carrying heavy weaponry.'

'T-12? Generally used for high-level official and military personnel.' I knew that much from previous dealings with them.

'Tumbling at two point oh-six rotations per minin,' his sub-officer confirmed. 'And it's bleeping the codes for non-aggression. And emergency.'

'But *why* is it on that exact trajectory?' I needed to know. 'Is this its original route? Or severely off course because of some collision, or internal problem?' We all had something to say – mostly voicing questions, rather than anything positive.

'We need to see if it's damaged; what the distress might be.'

'Or is this a ruse? To get closer to Fortex Base?'

'Can we stop their spin?'

My subs looked at each other when I asked, mandibles stiffening at the thought. 'Huge risk. Why would we?'

One shook his head. VC pulled a face. 'We'd need to see it closer, M'am; depends on mass, and tumble characteristics.'

'How long before we're able to communicate directly with it?'

More blank expressions. 'We're trying. Depends on the system they're using… if anything's working aboard her.'

'Can we blow it up before it gets close?' That's the safeguard.

'Yes, M'am, we could. But…'

'But what? You think she could be carrying novatron detonators? Enough to take us out, as well, if we let her come much closer? Better us than Fortex; that's why we're here.'

'Have the humans really got supernovs?' The Sub on the monitors sounded like the Eternal Pessimist from Eversafe4U.

'They've got them. And they've used them twice that I know to,' I said. 'We need to see it clearly, or contact it.'

Nav, Guns and Comms conferred briefly. 'Any moment, we should have visual from an out-monitor – Yes. Here.' They expanded the screen to facet-eye size. Precious little detail. 'Looks like severe damage down the length of her. One module shattered.'

'Any signs of life?'

'Nothing clear. No response to our probes.'

'This is no good to us. I need solid info. What's the possibilities of this being a tactical ruse?'

'Certainly a possibility, Commander. She could have a gyro-module near the centre of spin. It would negate much of the effects. Or using the roll as a false gravity alternative. Humans could live through that about as well as we could.'

'The roll is slightly less rapid,' Comms reported. 'Down to two per minin. That could mean she's being brought under control. Possibly their auto systems dampening-in.'

We all studied the screen and trigabytes of meaningless data.

'We *must* make contact,' I said, ever more exasperated as decision time crept closer. 'See if you can patch me through via the auto-voice link.'

Both subs objected to it being me who would attempt direct contact, 'I know the humans better than anyone. I'm fluent in Terrath and Stang. Yes, alright, Sub, so my accent is a little too shrill to ever sound native. But I know the people; I spent a lot of time there, remember?' *Wasn't a good time, though. Not at all.*

They nodded, prepared the links and antenna fittings, re-tuned, and I settled into the Comms Unit, let them wire me into the whole Eeth System. Strange, isn't it? You do the training, take all the memo-crysts, spend years on active duty, win your promotions and then you're stupid enough to put yourself in a position where it's all on you, not your team.

**

They brought me out eighteen mins later, with the usual blinding, prob-screwing headache. I say "usual", but I've only done it three times before, including two training

78

sessions, so it's not exactly commonplace. It takes a few moments to get your mind straight afterwards, while I considered what I'd learned.

'Right, I detected twelve living humans aboard. One is a female who I encountered previously. She was their Senior Negotiator at a peace conference; extremely determined; and absolutely dedicated to the Terrath cause.'

My subs demanded answers, guidance, directions, orders. Politely, of course. All highly anxious. Rightly so. 'Give me a moment,' I said. 'I'll remain rigged up so I can resume talks.' *Talks? Huh! I'm the commander of a war vessel, not a politician. I don't do "Talks". I use my initiative within the limits of my instructions and weapons.*

'Firstly, their increasing stabilisation is automatic, but not very effective—'

'We calculate they should be out of the tumbling about the same time they're at closest passage here. Think that's coincidence? Or planned? Certainly convenient, isn't it, Commander?'

That was true enough. Very convenient, and potentially dangerous to us if we allowed a stable craft to come that close. 'Only two survivors are crew, and they aren't Operations Crew, much less officers. The rest are passengers.'

'So they claim. Any proof?'

'No. It wasn't possible to sense around the interior. It's what they told me.'

'Purpose of travel in this direction?' Navs Cody was quick to get to the point.

'Armistice talks on Vrenh, they claim. But were hit by a cargo container that slipped out of its force-mesh. They

79

claim to have been like this for four days, confined to half the command floor; and no power other than emergency batts. They say they don't know where they're presently headed. Can we get confirmation of any of this? The talks? Or the incident?

Skyop drooped his spirick tubes in regret. 'I can't trace anything on the routine boards, M'am. And we can't enquire and receive an answer from Fortex in time. We'll have to decide ourselves.' *Won't you, Commander?* It was implicit in his words.

'Alright; the time is approaching. We know it might be carrying huge explosive power. We can't let it get close enough to us, or to Fortex Base to destroy us on a suicide intent. For Jogan's Sake, Calif, pull your wings in – you're an officer in the Arthroid Space Navy, not a tart on parade.'

'You think this could be a deliberate deception, Commander?'

'Of course, it could. We all know what humans are like – devious, determined, and deadly. Obviously, it could be a trick, we've been through that. They don't need to be a military ship to carry novatron bombs. If we allow them to close in on us, or on Fortex Base, then our whole defence system in this sector will be gone. We'll be wide open to their follow-up attack.'

'Do they do suicide attacks?' Weps Deeter could be naïve.

'Every time any of us – arthro or human – climbs aboard any ship, it's a suicide trip, Deeter.'

'Can we detonate them now? At this distance?'

'Just about. We'll catch some of the blast if they do have that kind of weaponry aboard. But we would survive. Most likely.'

'So do it, Commander. Give the word.'

How totally tempting to do exactly that. Rid the universe of her. Vaporise her, and all the rest of them. A kill so soon into my command would shine *so* bright on my Action CV, but... *'We can't.* Not just like that. *She's* aboard. She's *Senior* Jenntings. If she's genuinely on a peace conference mission to Vrenh, and we kill her – we'd blow up a protected vessel that's emanating emergency codes.'

'But it's heading directly into our restricted space. It's entered our territory already; doesn't answer our calls; and hasn't altered course as ordered. It shouldn't do that under *any* circumstances.' Sub-Cap Bard was beginning to look as desperate as I already felt.

'If they've lost all motive power, then they have no control of the circumstances.'

'Or pretending to be.' The command deck was feeling distinctly cooler. We all knew the angles on this. *Who'd ever trust a human again?* 'Evil, treacherous creatures.'

'They'll try anything. They have done in the past. Their word is nothing.'

'Members of peace contingents aren't renowned for being suicidal. Are they?'

I gave them a few minins so I could soak in all their possibilities and proposals; then called them to order through the melee of chittering and susurrating. 'I detected a fractional delay in my contacts.'

'So it's possible they might not be actually aboard?'

'Or it could be the effect of the rotation, seeking and losing the contact.'

I burred in agreement, 'Yes, it could be either.'

'You think it could be Holomats aboard? Projected in there?'

'Shugra! What do we do?'

'I've heard of Jenntings. If she really is aboard—'

'If?' I don't think even the humans would blow up their most senior peace staff—'

'Or would they? A martyr? To their cause? Think of her posthumous glory for destroying our Fortex Base. It'd leave us wide open.'

'You've met her, Mander?'

'Yes.' *Have I just.* 'At the Ghat Conference.'

'And before that, Commander? You said…?'

'She wasn't Senior back then, so it's not important.' *Damn you, Bard, don't get too persistent. I want no thoughts of Before That. Back when they betrayed our Treaty Mission. That was a ruse. And we fell for it. Hard to believe we were so innocent. Just twenty years ago.*

**

'This has been a blatant subterfuge… a terrible betrayal of the peace accord… an unforgiveable abuse of the white torch.' So spoke our President after his release, twenty-nine days later. 'The humans abused our goodwill… utterly flouted the agreement in order to obtain prisoners to torture and interrogate. They forcibly imprisoned our delegates to a Truce Forum.'

"Never trust a human" has been our watchword since.'

Only two of us survived, purely because our people rescued us. She was no Peace Commissioner then. She was a fanatic, even for a human. 'Yes, I think she's perfectly capable of sacrificing herself for the Great Cause.'

'Or they could be sacrificing her without her knowledge.'

'Or if she's just a holomat projection in there, no sacrifice is being made, anyway.'

'But,' I could see the other side, too, 'if that ship is truly going to the Accord Meeting at Vrenh, success at the table would be equally momentous for Terrath and Arth. And her personally.'

'If we detonate that ship—'

'Our base will be guaranteed safe.'

'How long for?' I said. 'See the bigger view. If we've destroyed their conference ship and peace staff? When they're already damaged and broadcasting the emergency codes? The war will take off anew.'

'With a vengeance. Literally.'

'So what the slimy shite do we do?' Shellric shrivelled his antennae helplessly.

'Sub,' I asked, 'can we get them off there?'

'And blow the ship afterwards? That what you're thinking?'

'Yes.'

'We could, but only if we put someone aboard with the pheetor unit. To act as the link. Yes, it might work, M'am. But that would tip them off about our capability with placement technology. And we absolutely do not want them to be aware of our capability there, much less get hold of it.'

'But, you *could* do it? Think it might work?'

'Ten percent chance, maybe. But who'd go? It would have to be… er…' They all looked at me.

'Commander? *You're* the only one who—'

'Yes. I know.'

Interrupted by Bard, 'But Commander. You have a history with Jenntings. More than you said.'

'So?'

'She was the officer who led that unit that took you–'

'You think I don't know?' *It was she, Jenntings, personally, who removed my first legs. All six. One at a time. Slowly. Twisting and ripping them off. Yes, absolute zealot.*

'I'm simply thinking, Commander M'am. Everyone knows it was her who tortured the prisoners. Including you. But—'

'But what, Bard?' I knew what he was going to say. *As if I haven't thought it a thousand times already.*

'Did she take something else?'

He had that tell-tale palp-curl, like when he's digging for something. *You would have to, wouldn't you, Bard?* 'Such as? What are you getting at, Bard? Come on – spell it out.'

He hesitated only a sec. 'Your free will. Your loyalty. You were with them a long time. Long enough to be Drained and Brained.'

I stared at him, glittered up my compounds a notch. 'And?'

'If *you* go, where does that leave us? I mean. If they turned you, Mander, when you were imprisoned – forgive me for saying – deep inside. Then you'd be safe on their craft. And you'd have our top technology with you, the pheetor unit. And it'd be perfectly possible for you to post a novatron bomb back to us.'

'We'd be left sitting here,' EN Raigh joined in, 'supposedly defending our Base, but leaving it wide open to whatever follow-up craft they've got coming down the line after their decoy.'

How strange, Bard. You have more sense and perception than you usually demonstrate. I've trained you well. I'd thought of that possibility many times since. Had Jenntings got into my head back then? That thought had niggled at me for almost two decades, and now it was coming to the surface. Was I turned back then? Had they – she – placed some key phrase to snare me? Is this their plan to obtain our pheetor technology? Rather than detonate our Fortex Base? Or as well as?

I was so sure I was fine. Until right now... *Am I rigged?*

'Well, Bard. Good thinking. It's up to you, then, isn't it? Your awareness of that possibility invokes Fourteen dot three – "In cases of doubt or incapacity". So it's up to you to decide. You and the rest of the Top Corp Team. That's regulations. Isn't it? I'm not permitted to order you to pheet me off-ship, and I can't log myself in and set the parameters to project myself and the unit to them. It's not physically or legally possible.'

He looked shocked at the result of his realisation – I would have allowed myself to be dispatched had he not raised the possibility of my traitority. Damn. I'd been so sure I was fine. Loyal? Of course, I'm loyal. I'm me. I hate the humans. *Don't I?* Now, I *must* hand the decision to them.

'So, gentlemen. The console's over there. What are you going to send? Me and the pheetor unit; or a novatronic bomb? I'll back you to the barrel-head whichever decision you take.

'Take your time. I estimate you have three minins to decide.'

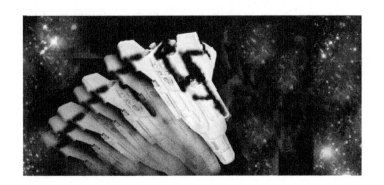

HOIST ON MY OWN HISTORY

'Grandad! There's going to be a lot of bother at the Star and Martyr today – they've taken on a Chari in the catering department. It's a real Octo-beetle, *here in Marrdiff.*'

The kids were excited to the floor and back – waving their arms in imitation of a Charipserid's multiple arm-flexing movement – incredible control of eight arms all at once. They had amazing control of all their tenty-arms even whilst locomoting – or walking and running, as we pretend to think of it. Yeah, right – four sets of arms and three sets of legs – the only impressive thing about them – their coordination. *Skauking beetle-shickers. Hate'em.*

Milly and Boone were obviously expecting me to be worked up about it – given my history with the Charis. *Alien filth.* But their news wasn't a surprise – I'd already heard that some of the building guys were fuffing up for a demo – and you know what their idea of a demo is. I was having nothing to do with it. Not going to demean myself by joining in. It'll get out of hand in no time. *If I go down there, I'll be at the front of the mob with a prise bar. Shicks – no way I'm going down there. I'm too worked up about'em already.*

'Oh?' I said, 'Really?' Feigning total disinterest.

'Yes, Grandad. You know all about them, don't you? You must go and see, mustn't you? After everything that happened—'

I stuck my hands up to quieten them. Buggerit, I'm hoist on my own history here – I *would* have to go. The kids expected it. All my past chuntering and hatred would take on a false face if I didn't at least go down there and smash it to a crunchy pulp. 'Maybe I'll wander down there with my cam.'

'Best take your EssGee as well, Grandad.'

'Maybe.' As I said, you know the building guys' idea of a demo: they'll scrat anybody who's not one of them.

'You might get a shot at the thing if they haven't ripped it apart by the time you get there.' I sometimes wondered about Milly's ideas of fun.

The choppy flight was all of ten minutes, and the mob was well up for it. I could see a morass of them spilling out the back of the Martyr – Yeah, the Chari was there – under a thrashing heap of fists and boots. Couldn't be having that. I dropped into them like the engine had blown – straight down on top of the whole melee. *That's scattered 'em,* I had to laugh. *Even gristlers like this lot never like to get diced and sliced by the extendi-blades – I put them on extra-length to keep them at bay.*

Twenty-odd seconds and the blades and my EssGee had the yard cleared – apart from the crusty that was scattered across the slabs – leaking and broken – like they all ought to be.

I dragged it out from under the rails. *Y' helpless,* I thought at it. *You're at my mercy. Shickit – the times I'd ached for a chance like this. I could have you in slices, you vile thing.*

But you won't. That's not in your mind. The damn creature was peering into my mind.

'Huh – think you can read all us humanics?' I felt like giving it a kicking for its presumption. Damn things always tried to tune in on our thinking.

It rattled. Something like a wheezing cough, leaking bluey-green fluid out of its sternum… upper thorax area. 'Most of you, we can, at least a little.' Couple of your segment plates are cracked – one ripped part out, the other caved in. The wheezing turned into a hack hack hack. The gruesome thing was amused at me. I felt like wringing its antennae twice round its neck – if it lived long enough.

'And you're surprised at the antagonism you lot get? Probing into our minds?' I knelt, to feel if the plates were loose. It let me.

'Surprised?' It shuddered, eyes closing in sequence; claw fists clenching. 'Not really – but with you, it's personal, isn't it? You can cover your mind. You've had close contact with us before.' One of its beaded glassy eyes widened and stared straight at me; trying to read me. I could block him… *it*.

'You don't need to read me to know that – I speak Semi-Pseudo language well enough for you to realise I've met your sort in the past.'

'Your accent's dreadful… Naporic Region? You were there in The Troubles?'

'Nothing to do with you where I was. Just shut up.'

It was having a lot of difficulty rasping a few words out. Good. Don't know why it bothered breathing any longer; it only said stupid things. 'You need patching. I'm no doc, but I've met enough arthrops to know how your panels and segments should be arranged. And yours aren't right – thorax's split open.' I checked round it.

'Couple of legs twisted, one snapped. Antenna crushed – stamped on, probably, when they got you down?

'What the Pit are you doing here on your own? Stupid thing to do. You must have expected bother?'

He ignored me; too busy wincing and arm-untangling while I tried to get fingertips under the shell-edge to pull the stove-in chest segment into place – the green gunge of his hemolymph smelled richly sour. 'Hold still,' I ordered him.

'You don't care for me any more than your friends do.'

'Shut the shick up – You're right, I don't care about you. But I am trying to care *for* you. And they're not my friends. They're also not stiffed off with me like they are with you.' *Soon will be, though, when they realise. Got to be quick here. Patch it first; then evack. Engine tape'll seal a couple of these cracks...*

'Just the same – you don't like us. Something personal?'

'Yeah – you exist.' I squeezed the segment inward and felt it click in position. He winced, rather pleasingly. 'You're not supposed to be aware of pain – so you can cut that out.'

'You obviously know we do feel pain. Where did—?

'Shut up.' I jerked and prised at a buckled segment. *That must hurt like shick. Extra-Good.* 'You can't stay here, Charlie Crust. Back yard of a bar isn't the place to treat anybody, even you.'

'So what are you? You hate us, but you crashed through them, took me into your charge, but...' He was attempting to delve at my mind: his tiric probe vibrated.

'That won't get you anywhere – I'm not penetrable beyond level one.'

'You're not police or guardiates. You just pretended to be. Just to get them off me? Why would—?'

'Shut it or I'll crunch your mandibulae – yes, yes, I know that's not how you speak – but it'd shut you up just the same.'

'So what are you going to do with me now?'

'What do you want me to do? And we'll see what's feasible.'

He considered. 'Return me to the Eresthan Hall.'

'Can't; this's just my personal choppy. It hasn't got the range, carrying two. You'll have to come back to my place till we get you right.'

'I'll call for rescue.' His eyes were fading. *Got to get a move on.*

'Don't be stupid. Your sending antennae are out. Let's get you clean… don't want you leaking all over the seats. Shicks – My kids are gonna love you.'

'You say that with great… irony? You mean the opposite. So why are you helping me?' His haemo was bubbling around the plate joints; the colour greening up.

'Why? How the Pit would I know why? Maybe so I can kill you myself. Not for love of *you*, personally, either. I hate *all* your kind. Come on, get in the choppy.'

By the time I'd loaded him into the floor space, I was sweating with the tension as well as the effort. But I had him out of sight, and tucked neatly in – a bit crunched-up, but wholly inside, and not splitting wider anywhere.

I was realising why he'd been there: he was a sacrifice. 'Why are you here? Risky place to be, the Malts.'

91

'I was allocated here. They said it was safe – much better relationships nowadays.'

'Yeah, right. Down here? In Marrdiff' I lifted the little choppy out the bar yard – two dozen angry faces below. A couple of the holding-back rioters threw something. Someone aiming a gun tube... a soft thud hit the choppy somewhere. *At least it wasn't a piercer or flamer.*

'And you were stupid enough to believe you were safe? *Down there? This part of town?* I can read you better than you can read me. You've no idea, have you?' His thinking was a dark swirl with muddy brighter patches among it – from which I garnered thoughts and beliefs – only the surface stuff that he couldn't help but let me see. Took no probing. 'You're a sacrifice – an incitement to bother. Your people have dumped you here to spark trouble – you're the price they're happy to pay to stop the accord going through. Someone on your side is, anyway.'

I could feel the depth of his shock at the thought, disbelieving. I was swooping the choppy northwards, glanced down at him as we leaned – Yes, he was coming to see its truth. Gradually sinking into his ganglionic masses.

'Do you have family?' – was my obvious next question.

He was aghast as realisation deepened. 'Yes... You think they could be in—' He choked off in a bout of hacking coughs that re-opened half the crusting joints.

'Koh – so where are they? Come on!' I wheeled the choppy round. 'Address? Exact? Landing spot? If nobody's got to them yet, you'll have to go in and bring them out to wherever I can settle her.'

Talk about a lack of trust. He'd been given accommodation in a compound with two other Charipserid families. Short hop across the rooftops. He was up on his joints, peering… then pointing to the tightest chopp-spot I've ever squeezed into.

Convinced I was going to dump him there, he was giving me the glass-eye until I told him, 'Shick off and see if they're all there and in one piece each.'

It was only when they all came clicking, beadying and antenna-swaying to the doors and windows to stare at me that I wondered what the fruggle I thought I was gonna do with them.

Absolutely nothing I can do for you all. I told myself. *My choppy carries two and one bag, at most.*

But out he came, staggering, clicking and confused – the trauma was getting into him. And his brood, by the looks of them.

'How do you usually travel? How'd you get here?'

'An old gyrobus. It's outside. We had a driver…'

A gyrobus in the back space. Maybe, then… 'You can all get in it?'

He twiggled his sirips in affirmation.

'Shuggs, this's gonna destitute me – or kill me.' I told him. *With a bit of luck.* 'You know how to drive it? What he does when he starts it up?' Even for a Chari, he was looking blank. 'Never mind… they're usually straightforward. Now – listen: I'm taking the choppy straight up – I saw a gathering in the streets about a frag away, heading this way – they'll have seen us coming in. I'll do a slam landing in the square back there – block the route, create a diversion. I don't run too fast, so I won't be back in seconds – it'll be minins.'

Disbelief, thy name is Charlie Charipserid. 'I *will* be back. So be ready to open up when I come hammering on the gates.'

My main problem wasn't crashing my choppy in the Marrdyke Square; nor turning the overheat on full. It wasn't even my so-called run back to the arthros' compound; nor getting the gyrobus started up – there's an under-dash short-circuit that'll do that. It was getting them to open up the shuggling gates.

A full five minins, I was standing there, gathering an audience that turned into a crowd and was building up to full mob status – when my choppy blew its zee tank a hundred yorkies down the avenue. The column of red-black smoke convinced everyone surrounding the house and gyrobus that something of more interest was amiss. En masse, they chose the guaranteed fire-cracking entertainment, and dashed off to my choppy's funeral pyre.

Out they came, then, the Charis. Like a disgorging nest of giant insects – beetles – Charipserids. That's exactly what they are, I suppose. Eighteen of them. One lot greeny-blue, the others more of the dark golden. I never had figured out the difference – something to do with status or heritage or origin. I never cared before and I wasn't going to worry now.

Chirruping and chittering – lot of suppressed panic among them; lot of confusion. But they were doing what Crusty Charlie had told them. He'd persuaded them. I must have convinced him, maybe that I was their only hope.

The gyrobus was too wide to get it down any of the streets where I live, and there was no way I could pretend I didn't have nearly twenty beetles – all as tall as me – living in my apartment. 'It'll have to be Beetle Hall,' I told them.

And that was a long, very circuitous journey to leave Marrdiff township by a non-direct route and circle round to the Eresthan compound, where the visitors' official delegation was based.

'How did you know?' Charlie came round to the cab when I pulled into their yard. 'That we were sacrifices?'

I knew I had to tell him. He needed to know it was true. 'Experience. All the signs are there. It's what my lot did with me. I was placed on a farmstead on Naporia. The district was guaranteed friendly. We'd been there twenty-one days when they came. *The Massacre*, it was called. Your lot dropped on our four families – slaughtered everyone, tore them apart, alive... dissected them – my wife. And my youngsters – in their twenties, but still my kids.'

He had that totally blank look that usually means disbelief with their lot.

'I was at a government meeting, discussing trade arrangements and how we were being threatened. No-one was taking it seriously. Mostly, I think they wanted to believe that things were going well, and weren't listening to us. It brought the Troubles to a head, alright – Lot of blood and hemo spilled after that. Only two of our whole mission survived – and Kenzie didn't live long after he got back – killed himself. Not that I saw any of it: they kept me in the Block House – you know it? The grey building off Union Square? It's true – how many floors of cellars it's got. They had me in there two years, till the Access Agreement.'

I shut up – too choking with the memories. I'll never be free of the rawness, I expect. 'If you're going to head off your very own *Massacre*, you need to root out whoever placed you there. Some dissident group among your opposition, most likely. That's what it was with us. Integration needed more time – and less antagonistic early placings. Better, more tolerant, forward-looking suburbs.'

'But you have kids… you said.'

'My grandchildren – they were due to join us later.'

'But you survived okay?'

'Did I? I chirrup some nights, and I'm pretty sure I have three thoracic plates forming. Sure, I survived. I'm *really* integrated.'

I'LL TAKE THE LITTLE ONE ON THE END

'The little one. I'll take the little one on the end. What is it?' As if I don't know.

'But Majesty—' My Persona Advisator spoke. And stopped abruptly at the raising of my fore-claw.

'It is decided, PA. I have made my choice.'

Fool. The scraggy creature is among your group of ten that I must choose from; therefore, I can pick whichever one I wish to. Even if it's only included to make up the obligatory number and species mix.

PA clearly wasn't liking it, but so what? 'Your role in providing the choice is ended. Mine is begun with making my choice. It's made. Now proceed with our coronation.'

It's a human, of course, I know what it is, although this is the first one I've seen in the, er, flesh – closer than a vin-screen away. *You're a dilapidated looking thing, aren't you? They sure brought you into the line-up as a chuckaway.*

'Yes, that's decided,' I repeated it, louder, to make sure they all heard me; and to affirm to myself what I'd done. 'The off-planet thing on the end. I'll have that one.'

The constitution requires that the new Regina shall choose her pair-mate from "a broad spectrum of available specimens and species". It gives the immigrant communities the idea they're equally in the running for power. As if.

I saw the whisper go along the line of my ceremonial team. 'She's chosen one of the aliens… That thing on the end.'

Somewhat amusing, but, beyond assembling the ten for me to choose from, my advisators have no further say in the matter. They obviously had one definite preference at the fore. Right in the middle, and glory-decked for the occasion – a fellow *Aytathian* – *big, undoubtedly handsome. A vacant sort of expression – yes, he'd be easily controlled by them. Probably superb in his mating habits. They think that would sway my decision? They plan to mould me? Through a beauty-boy like that one they've trained? Think again.*

A couple of other Aytathians stand there, one each side of him, whom my advisators might find acceptable, if suitably trained up and bullied into shape.

Looking again along the row of non-favoured offerings, none of this straggly string of sorry misfits was even in the race. Yurk – what a collection, looking totally lost and bewildered. They most likely had no idea why they were there, quite possibly criminals, disposable miscreants of all available species, including, I imagine, the maggoty human thing.

I certainly wasn't going to pair up with the bristly scorpioid, or the multi-tentacled jellyball on four pseudo-legs from Minu. These different species are usually passing through one of the terminal ports, and get stranded, or decide they've come far enough. A veritable melting pot nowadays, Aytath.

Zoogs above! My advisators and officials are trying to hide their aghastness, but failing. I allow myself a small smirk. I make no attempt to hide it, of course.

So now, I am committed to this repulsively squishy little alien. Even from this distance, it looks smelly and dirty in clothes and body – probably in mind, as well. *I'll show them they're not the only ones who know how to coerce underlings into shape. I can do the same thing with the little humanic-alien. It doesn't look strong enough to resist, physically or mentally. They'll see what training is. There. That's it. I've made my choice and they must abide by it.*

I spend a moment smugly gazing around the assemblage of the Advisator Panel; the government and state officials; the bizarre bodies and bewildered minds of the selected candidates. Mmm, I permit myself another grim little smile, taking in the wide stage, the last few hangings of decoration waiting to be raised in time for my imminent coronation, or, in theory, *our* coronation – me and my... *thing.* Not to mention the audience of The Chosen Witnesses – One gross and one Aytathians to represent the people of Aytath. My people, who will vouch that this has been done.

You expect me to rule? Right. This is my choice of partner. You pack of failures. I twirled a pair of fluffings in disgust at their blatancy and abject failure. I am The Divine Regina who can do no wrong, and who has access to higher levels of understanding than they have. Huh – if mine's superior, theirs must be awfully low.

They shall not manipulate me, as they did my mother, and her mother before. As from yesterday, I rule. As Regina, it's possible for me to think these things. I'm entitled to engage in internal rebellion.

'Majesty,' Tsig concurred. As he had to. That made me smile again. I do little smiling since I knew my time as Regina was upon me. Would I dare to pick one of the Unchooseables; and thus defy their wishes? The festering human was the least likely anyone would choose – the utterly impossible one. Wretched little maggot.

Yes, I'm relieved that I've dared to do it. Though what will happen next, beyond the coronation, is a mired unknown – huge challenge ahead. No Regina has ever chosen a member of the minority alien species before, much less the eleventh option out of ten. Good reason to permit myself yet another inward smile.

'Bring it to me.'

It stumbled, as a heavily-crested and garbed guard bellowed in its audio-flaps from behind, and pushed it forward. Struggling back onto its legs – *Only two – I suppose that's good – it shouldn't get itself tangled up as frequently as the seggies do. Clumsy igiots.*

It took a few sharply-prompted steps towards me. Yes, a human. Some similarities of morphology with we Aytathians – small head at the top with sensory and communicatory organs clustered there. Thorax and abdomen. Plus arm and leglike appendages for grasping and locomotion. But only two of each. And, actually, it seemed to be limited to two of everything – visual and auditory sensors – nostril cavities…

Weird indeed, though nothing like as revolting as some of the others in the line-up, like the lump-ugly toader from Wherever. And as for the awful smell of the piscine at the other end… or the gills'n'frills hooyuck that had been next to him – Yurk. Not the most alluring bunch I've ever seen.

Hmm, I sensed bewilderment as it was escorted close to me. Motioning all others to step back, I spoke to it quietly. 'You are chosen,' I told it. It didn't react. Are humans deaf? Or utterly stupid. 'Do you understand?' The thing stood there, insignificant. *You're going to take some training at this rate.* But I'd known that since the whole idea of defying the advisators had come to me. 'You have permission to speak.'

'Chosen for what?' Ah, it did speak. It understood. Something in its favour at last. Somewhat husky in tone, though, and the accent! Where did it learn that? Milberdown? 'Chosen for ritual execution, am I?'

Do you really think that? Do you not know? Or is this some attempt at alien humour? Must read up on your habits and mores, now I have you, little creature. 'You're to be my partner. I am the new Regina.'

The feeling that emanated from it was one of disbelief and amusement, uncertainty and defeat, not utter joy. 'Can't you pick the big Aytathian in the middle? Much more your type. They've been fussing round him all day. He's all prepped up to be decapitated, crowned, or whatever.'

Ah... confirmation of their intentions from the oral cavity of a human. 'We'll discuss it later. In the meantime, we need to get you cleaned up, less stinking, and... Tangalone knows how we'll get clothes round a body like yours.' It listened, and looked baffled, so I repeated it slowly, with gestures, sensing greater confusion from it. *Have I really, profoundly clonged in this choice? The carapace one with the colour of fire was my second choice...* But no. The human it would have to be. *You can meet with a nasty accident if things aren't working out.* I motioned to Siggy and told him of my clothing requirements for my human.

'Come, creature, we need to speak further whilst you are being prepared.' I claw-clicked at Siggy, 'Clothes for it. Now.'

'That bad, is it? For me?'

I wasn't certain of its mood in that voice, but it didn't sound too respectful or joyful.

Hmm. You're going to be trouble, alright. The next banquet may well have a new, humanic-shaped, centrepiece down the top table.

It caught my look, 'You made it sound like you're getting me plucked for Sornday Dinner.'

'Mmm. Hold that thought in mind, little one. If you cross me, you won't be able to complain you weren't warned, will you?'

It stared back at me – most rudely – and muttered something.

'Come,' I grasped one of its arm things, 'we shall speak in the Robing Room.'

Uckinfell. What have I got into this time? Looking round this room, it's like a vid-star's changing room – there's lights and clothes hanging everywhere – and things that look like frill-crimpers and tentacle-plumpers. *I really can't get into this – I gotta go.*

Or have I? Maybe I can lie low here for a time? Although this situation isn't exactly out of sight and mind if the Fed come looking for me.

This thing's a female – no, they don't got tits – not in the right place, anyway. They're taller and thinner than the males, and got two rows of neck frills. "Riding a double-necker," they called it, having sex. That's what I overheard when I was in a bar one night, anyroad.

'I've never spoken with a human before,' she trilled at me. 'You don't stray this way too often.'

'Me? I'm a stray wherever I go, Lady of Aytath, but I've never strayed this way before. And I don't think I had any idea where we were heading, or even where this is. Not that I cared much. Anywhere would have done, the state we were in.' I wasn't feeling too sociable, after the last few days I'd had. Uckaflone knows what this is about.

Something on her head perked up, might have been a sort of nostril affair. Or maybe not. 'And why would that be?' she said.

She needn't start inquisiting me. 'Mind your own,' I told her. 'Yurghhh!' She only had me flat back on a table among all these body decoration things, with a set of double claws round my throat.

'You're polite to me. Or you're dead to me.' It was a sort of hissy rasping voice she had then, from a hand's length in front of my face. The back of her throat was a sight I'll never forget.

Well, that was telling me, alright. I'd have told her to uckfoff but I couldn't breathe, much less cuss her. So I just struggled, 99% ineffectually, and sort of sank when my air supply dropped below zero. That really pissed her off. She must have thought I was doing it deliberately, and she wasn't going to permit me to droop and die quietly. Looger! She loomed even closer, and I thought for a moment she was going to do the kiss of life with me. That scared the shit of me, I tell you.

So there I was, on the floor – nice bit of Arellian parquetry, I noticed – getting some air back in my lungs. Screw me up the Yoogles! It had been a bad time since we left Kisjob – six of us on the Redit Cargo. "Disreputable and criminalistic", we were described as on the bulletins. Phew – that was putting it mildly for two of my oppos, Sindi and Lu – both known to be multi-murderers of humans and some other species I don't know. At least I was only known as a thieving, mugging arsehole, but that's only because I'm more careful about my ID when

103

I'm doing naughty things round the spaceways. I imagine my kill-tally is as high as Sindi and Lu's put together.

Okay, we tried to hijack a yacht-racer coming out the terminal on Jyath. Shuggs – what a cock-up that was. They panicked – the yacht lot – and didn't look where they were accelerating to – straight into, and damn-near through – a passenger cruiser coming in.

We were out of there soon as. In all that mess and muck, we screwed out and made for the hills, as they say – as far and fast as. The reward for us is something phenomenal – price on our heads, balls and boobs.

Sixth or seventh planet, and we call in here. Need a hujen unit, so I get sent into the town to find one at the yappers and scrappers, and they said they deliver and collect payment at the same time. So I stop off for a drink on the way, get delayed by a second drink, and… you know how it goes. And when I'm back at the pad, the Redit's gone.

I ranted and raved for around half a minute, till it occurred to me that nobody'd bother with just me – it was the ship and them lot they'd be after. Unless, of course, Sindi and Lu tipped the wink to the Fed that it was me who was piloting when we shot off, from Kisjob, and they could find me here, stranded. Fat chance of keeping my head down and waiting it out if I got to partner up with Aytath Ayleen here. Ha! Regina, indeed.

I looked up at it – bloody sharp claws she had; and neck frills like a razor shark. 'Not one to cross, are you, Lady?' I told her. 'Never seen any of you before I landed here; plenty since, and I'm not impressed.'

I managed to stand up after a bit, coming nearly up to her frilly bits – quite spectacular they are, too. *Can't be having this*, I thought, bossed and bullied by a banded bayack from Aytath – I mean, who ever heard of Aytath?

No, I got to make a stand, so, when I got myself steady, I told her, 'Listen scaley one, I killed around a thousand souls – humans, fragoes, piscies, seggies and all sorts. And that's just this year. So one more won't make much difference, Aytath tart or not. Queeny or queery. So wucking fotch it.' There, got to lay it out, an't you? If she can't take it, maybe she'll slice me up – that'd be quick – better than lingering on this pit-of-a-planet being screwed round waiting for the Fed. 'So come you tentacled tart – let's get this sorted.'

Scruggit! She was cross. Lashed at me. But that was so obvious, I ducked and whammed her one in the – whatever that segment between belly and thorax is, where it's soft as sogg-bread. She uffed forward – folk usually do when they get a good one in that area. She din't expect that, not from me, and I din't expect to get her quite so solidly. Talk about taking the wind out of her.

So we both end up on the floor this time, and she's urgghing for air worse than I had been, 'What you doing here?' she's gasping in the poshest accent I ever heard in any language.

Purely for contrast, I kept up my Gutter dialect version of Aytath – or hers was most likely some high-class local version of Uni-stang – but not the variety I know and abuse.

'Doing here? Engine trouble, came down for spares and repairs. I got myself into a bit of bother in a bar when somebody didn't like the look or sound of me – probably both. I was winning till I got lectro'd and charged with riot. No wonder you don't get many humans here – treat us like that.

'This morning, they made me take a memo-burst for the language. "So you can understand the charges," they said. And I found myself in a bloody line-up on stage. Never been in one on a stage before.'

Eckinfull; for me that was a speech. It was disappointing there wasn't a drink within reach on the floor. 'So, what you going to do, exactly? With me, I mean?'

She turned her eyes to me – huge iridescent ones in a row across her head. Obviously weighing me up.

'Well?' I said, getting impatient with her. 'What have you got lined up for me? Come on, before I go into D.O.'

'What's D.O?'

'Declining Orbit – the big burnup. Like when you know you're done and there ain't no getting out of it. I'm heading that way – look at the state of me – flattened under a shelly alien so I can hardly breathe.

'You mean you aren't always so filthy, haemoid-splattered, patchily-coloured, violent, rude and ignorant?'

'Well, I am, yes. Possibly not so blood-bedecked, but the other things, yes. This's about average.'

So then she's giving me the silent, multi-facet stare. So I breaks the moment and tells her, 'I think you have the most beautiful eyes I've ever seen,' mostly meaning it, but a bit of flattery doesn't do any harm – unless you're a Gedfer, of course. Which she isn't.

'Oh,' she says, 'which ones?' And she flashes up with another row just above the neck frills area. She only did it for effect, showing off. 'They are like this because I'm The Regina.' She was using them to extra-study me. That felt weird, like being interrogated by a pack of Bandrig wardens.

'You have a lot of fingers,' she observed. 'Eight, plus thumbs…'

'You got just as many,' I retaliated – I recognise a sneery tone when I hear one. 'They're just spread round four armicles instead of two proper arms.'

She did this sort of vibration of these little antennae they have on the top – where real people have hair. 'That was slightly amusing,' she said. 'Do you do it on purpose? Try to upset people? Because it'll not work with me. If you get funny with me, you'll be the Sornday Roast, I told you.'

'Yeah, well, as long as I'm dead first. I got no future anywhere else.'

'You could have. Behave, and you'll be my companion.'

'Slave?'

'Eventually, you might become my junior lackey, though you'd be known as my Regent.'

'Equals?'

'Don't be absurd.'

'Arm Candy?'

'You're being ridiculous again. Have you seen yourself?'

And have you seen yourself, I thought. *Sitting on the floor of a robing room, and still got a bit of a gasp-for-breath air about you, arguing with somebody like me. You're not looking entirely like a winner yourself.*

'I scrub up,' I told her, and pushed my hair back a bit. Course, the awkward bloody stuff sprang straight back. 'And I'd have to behave?'

'Naturally; can't have you—'

'I don't do behaving. Or lackeying. Better sharpen the carving knives.'

107

She did the vibration bit again – thought something was amusing. 'I picked you, as the least likely to make my advisators happy. And as someone I can mould to my requirements.'

'Ahh, moulding… Sorry, that's something else I don't do. And your requirements for what? Exactly?' She was reaching up to the neck frills, raking claws through them and making a right pigra's back-end of it.

'Here, let me,' I said and reached up, finger-raking through them. I think the shudder that went through her was shock – at being touched, I imagine. 'So what are you, then? The new boss round here?'

'Yes. The Queen. The Regina. The whole planet is under my governance – or it will be when I'm coronated.'

'Crowned? And when's that?' I raked a bit more, wondering how sensitive the frilly bits were, and if I grabbed them and screwed them up, would she be malleable PT in my grip, or would she retaliate and pincer my hands off at the wrists? *Best save that voyage of discovery for later,* I decided.

'As soon as we leave this room. They're putting the finishing touches to the décor, and assembling the guests.'

'Like I'm putting the finishing touches to you?' I dug my nails in a mite harder, round her sort-of-throaty bit. The greenish tips were deepening up, and I wondered what that meant. *This isn't a bit of foreplay, is it? I could offer to let you play with my bits, if you want to reciprocate? Maybe that's another thing best left until later?*

'Is this embarrassing for you? Me doing this?'

'There's no-one watching. So not at all, really. Not really.'

So it is. 'You want help washing and grooming? Dressing?'

'Don't be preposterous. Just get off me and stand up. This is undignified.'

'Not if we're in private; you just told me that,' I said, struggling to my feet and giving her a hand as she untangled her legs and armicles to stand.

So there we stood – both of us wondering what the chuff to do next, how to go for it, I suppose. So I leapt in, seeing as she didn't seem to be on the cusp of a negotiating proposal. 'Okay, Scissorhead—' She bristled at that, but I carried on, 'What is it you want from me? And don't say just to piss them lot off. You've got to have specific reasons – or can think of something. Suppose I cooperated – what would you want?'

That stilled her. Then she turned to a mirror and started re-grooming herself. I imagined that was what all the fiddling about was, while she presumably thought about it.

And I was thinking if I'm in this situation, I'd better make the best of it – it's preferable to be high profile and comfortable, rather than sozzed out my mind, and gutter'n'bar dwelling. 'You put me up there with you, and give me some say in which humans come to Aytath – like anybody except the Fed.'

She was half-listening while she self-groomed or whatever she was doing. To be honest, I wasn't certain how much of what I could see was her, and how much her clothing.

'What I want from you?' That was when I found out which bits were clothes, and which bits were her. She was quite something like that – the scaly-frilly neck gave way to a downy thorax – and the bit where I'd landed her one was fully exposed now. The rest was a tangle of legs and unmentionables that I wasn't inclined to learn about. Not then. *Not in any lifetime,* I remember thinking. *You are sorta smart, though.*

'It occurs to me,' she said, 'that the few humans we do see arriving here are well-off – present company discounted, of course. They spend money, and there is potential in expanding—'

'Expanding your Gimme-Pockets?'

'Exactly. You think you could take on some responsibility for matters regarding humans?'

Now, I'm accustomed to thinking on my feet, thinking fast, and going full hick for whatever I decide. So there I am – *we* are. *She's pretty much the same as me,* I'm reckoning. So, I stuck my neck into the blender, 'There're positive sides to a job like that; and there's negative ones, as well. If we're on confess'n'brag time here…?'

'We could be.' She sounded somewhat dubious about that; got a lot at stake, I suppose. But no more than me.

'Sure, I could do things on the positive side – encouraging, build up trade and investment – it was my line, originally – seems like a century back – PR, sales, marketing, anything in that line. But, of late, I been much more on what people regard as the negative side of life.'

'You're saying…?'

Ahh, she's interested. Must be stirring up her benthic depths. 'Okay, Lady – shit, I can't keep calling you Lady – what's your name?'

'Majesty.'

'Ock fuff.'

'Regina,' she tried

'It'll be Vagina at the rate you're going.' So, of course, she looked baffled – I think: it's not easy to tell baffled from entertained with the Aytaths. 'Make the next one acceptable, or I'll be calling you Droopy.'

110

I think it was the hard, hating, shall-I-slice-its-head-off look that she treated me to, before she capitulated, 'Megah. I'm Megah. I never—' She changed her mind about saying more. Just as well.

'Okay. In private, I'll call you that if we agree on things here, hmm?' I wasn't waiting for an answer; it's usually best to assume a "yes", and carry on. 'In the meantime – On the negative side, I'm wanted, preferably very dead, by the Fed. I'm held responsible for around eighteen hundred deaths, boosted by an unfortunate collision on the spaceways recently, but that's just my sort-of career climax, really.'

Isn't it just? You get cheated once; and blamed; and convicted and incarca-fucking-rated. So you y' make your heroic bid for freedom and steal a space-gig – it was only a little one – and someone gets their stupid self killed jumping on the off-gantry just as I've dropped her into max-drive. And it's all down the gravity well from there.

Being a scum-crook, a killer, must have been my calling. I just didn't realise it. Never looked back – "Once you set foot on that dusty road, my boy..." I hacked up the pontificating idiot who said that.

'I'm prepared to do whatever's necessary, positive or negative, to get you what you want; and you do the same for me.'

'And you want?'

'New ID, name, facial surgery... plus whatever luxurious accoutrements accrue with being your regent. You want a few of your underlings, advisators, officials and suchlike removed from time to time? I can do that. Ease them aside, or bury them – whatever. And I have very substantial ideas on how to get Aytath on the much-

111

visited track of The Great God Humanic Tourism. Trade? Deals with various humanic planets – I have contacts – devious, dubious ones, yes, but we understand each other.'

She looked interested – I think that look was "interested".

'I will back you,' I promised, 'solidly and proactively. I don't do orders-following all the time, I'm more into initiative. So, some of the time, I'd front you, not just back you.' There. That was it. Me, palms up. 'I'd stay back; nothing in public you don't want. But, when you're okay with it, I get the pseudo-surgery.'

'That'd upset the council.'

'What?' I asked, 'My face? Trade increased a thousand percent in the first year? Or their numbers being halved?'

It was definitely a smile; the twirl of her eye-letri confirmed it. A long hesitation while her mind expanded on the possibilities. 'Shall we discuss some of the details while we help each other dress?'

I twisted my thoracids in unexpected anticipatory pleasure with the way things were going with this human. We discussed further; tried on some new clothes; the official fine ones for me; and some that Siggy brought from the stores for him – previous occupiers probably dead, one way or another. We made some mention of possible socio-sexual partners of our own species... what individual freedoms we might allow each other... what *imaga publicca* we would present. *Friggatoré – he is quite something on the ideas and planning front.*

I am not stupid: I studied him as we talked and negotiated, sorted through the clothing, and upped my ambitions as we seemed to meld our minds more closely. I tried to kid myself that I had seen something in him when I first saw him. But no – I fool myself – it was by sheer contrariness that I chose him – a weak-looking thing that I'd hoped to mould to my ways of irritating my advisators.

As we continued, we were coming to agreements – I swore inside to each one, and meant it. And so, I think, did he.

'Come,' I eventually said. 'Let me look at you, my Regent. Let me see that you are fit and decorous enough to be at my side.'

Yes, I smugged within, *You'll do. Very nicely.* 'Come, Lord Regent.' I held out to him, 'Shall we go to our coronation?'

And there we went, hand in tendrifrill, me and the little one on the end.

PLAN B

Regional Controller TD White instantly donned his ultra-impatient, blazing-mad not-you-again look as soon as the screen cleared, and he confirmed that it actually was me – the accursed nuisance from Negeet. Seeing that expression, I shut my mouth and waited – he was obviously going to speak, and carry on speaking – ranting – before I could squeeze a word in.

'What is it *this* time, Gragg?' Norg Almighty! Was he in a mood. 'And it better be good. Or else. This better not be yet another digup on your property. So make it good, Gragg.'

This was going well. Everybody else I screenup is at least polite, and they wait until I've spoken before reacting; and they call me Mr Gragg, or Yeffy. But TD's the Regional Controller, ultra-busy, super-impatient and super-self-important. As much as anything with him, it's because he suspects his wife is on The Game and he's permanently short of temper, and manner. She is – everybody knows that much for sure. But I didn't mention that. I didn't need to right now. *Save it for a better occasion,* I thought. Not that she's been with me, I hasten to add – Marietta and I are perfectly happy as we are. So are the endless children who seem to cluster around me whenever I screenup long distance – they like to make snide comments to put me off my stride when I'm chatting live. They're lovable like that.

'It keeps you on your toes, Dad,' they say. Who'd have'em, eh?

'Er—' was all I managed to get out before TD interrupted.

'It is, isn't it? You dug up yet another something else? How many times do you need telling?'

'Er, yes. This one's—'

'—exactly like all the rest. Yes - like every other find you've had in those three norging fields. How many finds is it? Eighteen this year? Just in three plots. What's this one? Bigger? Shinier, smoother, more sticky-outish like cannon? Not singing and dancing, is it? *It was a battlefield*, for Norg's sake. You expect to find relics. It's what you're there for – clearing the rubble and trees and any wreckage you find. Get it in your thick norging head – I don't want to know about every single scrap of Yerrick debris you find. Nobody wants to know. How many times do you need telling?'

'But it could be important, TD—'

'You tell him, dad.'

''Shuffle off, Yoli,' I aimed a clout at my youngest… youngest of the walking ones, anyway. I don't count the others.

'Gragg! The battle in your area was two hundred years ago. There's nothing of value. It was all ploughed-over and buried not long afterwards, in the Big Clearup.

'Every time you screen me, it's the same old, same old. Every time, you're telling me, "This is the one". No, it's not. It's yet one more different bit of some duo-century-old smash-up. And there'll be more. And others after that. Do whatever you want with whatever it is. Break it up. Dig it out. Open a tourist stopover with integrated toilet. Sell the metal. Another pulverised screw-bolt off a lift unit, is it? Or an intact Class One Deadweight-Battlecruiser Pride of the Imperial Spacefleet?

'I don't want to know, Gragg. Nor does Regional Council and the Heritage Committee. There's no interest. It's yours. A bonus. All you have to do is clear this year's allocation of land – three plots to make useable for agriculture. And you need to get that done or you're out the exitway with no reserve.'

I signed off then. Actually, I signed off about five seconds after TD had cut the link.

'That went well, Dad,' my cluster congratulated me. Sarcasm is their big new word this week.

'What you found this time, Dad?' Ginita, my eldest manages to sound derisory even with what seems like an innocent question.

'Another cannon that turns out to be an axle off a clearancing kosho?' Maykti liked to practise her sneery lip.

I growled and they scattered and we all laughed. We had this understanding like that – They did the jokes and I screwed things up. And none of us told Marietta the truth about anything.

But the kids, of course, know everything. Think they do, anyway. And, mostly, I suppose, they do. It's like Us versus the World, and we make a game of it.

'Like I told TD the RC, I was deep-ploughing along the wide-strip that's due to be the new roadway this morning – please stop doing that, Cygmund – and I hit something, so I'm out the cab and checking and it's the usual white-satin metal that fetches a price with the yippies.'

'But it's big and smooth and still a bit shiny under the mud,' They all chanted it – my usual litany to TD.

'Ah, my sarky little fruit-of-my-loin,' – they didn't like to be reminded of their origins – 'what I didn't get

117

round to telling him is that this is interior, not outer hull. Some unit from inside, and it's not one of the reinforced heavy-metal gunnery things… or engine shielding.'

'You always say that, Dad.'

'I bet it's another drive motor cowling.'

I had to shake my leg to clear them away.

'Dad, you can't spare the time to be fiddling about unearthing another bit of smashed-up rubble.'

'You've got to finish the clearancing before the season's ended.' Full of helpful thoughts, they are – bright-eyed without the bushy tales

'Drag it out, roll it down the hill to where the yippies'll collect it for scrap.'

'But—'

'No, Dad, it's not a tri-valent bomb. They didn't have'em then, Dad.' Jerimia, Number Two, was super-patient with me sometimes.

'I got a feeling—'

'You've always got a feeling.'

'That's what Mum says, too.'

'Just finish the plot; it's got to be clear by season's end.'

'Or tidy up the far plot.'

'I can't. I need to clear this strip first, or there's no allocation for next year – TD RC made that clear enough. So this thing has to come out.' There, that was decided. I smiled broadly round them all. The suspicion on their little faces! Who'd have untrusting kids, eh? Marietta's influence, of course.

Then Jenny-Dee comes up with her bright idea – the one I'd sort of mentioned in passing while we were coming back from our latest find, 'Why don't you let us take a few days off our usual edu-work schedule, and we could do the finishing on far field while you—'

'Couldn't dream of it,' I protested. 'Marietta would never—'

'Dad, dad, dad,' they clamoured, 'you must.' Oh good. Seed planted nicely, Jenny-Dee and me. So that was decided upon. It'd take them off the infilling and colly-stud work they didn't like.

'Just don't let your mother know; not yet, anyway. If she asks, you're doing your routine stuff—'

'And you're investigating your latest two-hundred-year-old bomb.'

'Just don't tell y'ma things like that. I have to pick my moments for that kind of news.' As if that was going to happen – it was written all over Yolanya and Mixita that they were going straight round to snitch on me. Ah well, I already beamed it to her, so she could put on her act. As long as TD Arsy doesn't find out.

Getting late, but I might as well get the short-arm digger on site and in position for an early start on the morrow. Ginita came with me and we thought we might as well just have a little dig all the way round the thing, see if we could estimate the size of the job. Maybe get the sluicer up there, too and wash it down a bit.

So it was somewhat late and dark when we staggered back home – weary but happy, as that revolting little cartoon guy always says – and shared the info with all and sundry while we cursed the doyogs for eating our suppers.

'Dad,' I'd primed Ginita, 'There really isn't anything different about this one.'

'I got a feeling,' I said.

And the kids and Marietta said, 'You've always got a feeling.' And we were laughing about it and we found something warm in the oven – it looked like Charlie's doyog from down the next plot. But what the heque? Tasted fine.

'One day – you see,' I told'em, and we all laughed again.

I was thinking about that new find up there on the wide strip. I just knew there was something about it when I first found it a couple of days ago. And looking at it this evening with Ginita, cleaning some of the mud off, and feeling it. It wasn't exactly common knowledge that a Battleweight Cruiser had come down in this vicinity. That's because not many people these days are in the least interested in the goings-on of two hundred years earlier, in the pre-settled days. But it's definitely known among those who are interested in such things. It was a spaceship – never intended to land anywhere. But it had suffered a fatal hit, and lost its orbit. Almost certainly broke up on its way down. Dozens of big bits were scattered in this region, and hundreds of small ones.

This particular section didn't look especially familiar, but which part of a two-hundred-year-old alien spaceship does? Even on the supposedly reasonably accurate plans and schematics of the interiors of such craft, I couldn't spot anything similar. But what blueprints of enemy warships ever are?

Shiny and smooth, with knobs on. And several broken pipes coming from it, 'Or going to it,' Ginita reminded me. A bank of dials – all shattered; and cooling grids that were buckled and smashed flat. Several ports and weld points showed where other things had fitted to it.

From the portion that was exposed during the evening, we were thinking in terms of a pod of some kind, perhaps a communications unit... Or air con... Power? Heating? Weapons control?

'With a full day's digging out, it should be possible to identify it to some degree.' Ginny sagely informed me.

'Yes dear.'

'It needs to be dug out and removed anyway, Dad. You can't leave it here if the new roadway's following this route.' Yoli knows these things.

'Yeh, yeh, I know.' I was muttering and nodding to myself, not displeased that Yoli had decided to come along. She's a bright girl.

'Dad,' she said. 'Have you put your hand on it? Felt it?'

'Mmm,' I said. 'I have. You can feel it, too?'

'Dad? It's still live, isn't it? Something's still ticking.'

'I don't know about ticking, Yoli. It's like ticking without the ticking. Something is live – there's power of some kind remaining in there. Are you staying to help? We'll need to get on with it if we want to have it done today.'

We were finished mid-afto, and stood on the muddy rim of our new pit, gazing down at the gleaming metal unit we'd unearthed. 'It's a module, Dad.'

'A podule. Too small to be a module.'

'Nearly as big as the digger. More broken-up. Lot of smooth, unbuckled parts. Could it be a weapons unit? The sort that's independent in case of attack? Like a sealed-in controller?'

'He'll be fed up if he's still inside.' We looked at it and felt at it, and considered it and left it there for the night. 'I'll go down to the yippies and fetch some sensors. You want to come with me?'

No, she didn't. 'Right. And we'll test it tomorrow, hmm?'

'There's possibly something still live,' we continued next morning. 'Not *alive* – a long-period battery.'

'Probably taking power from the ambient temperature.'

Ginita and Yolanya made their pronouncements, 'It's probably nothing.'

'I'd best inform TD Arsy.'

'No! Dad, no. You can't. He told you—'

'But this could be important. I have to inform him.' *And if he tells me to effoff the airwaves, then I'm free to do with it as I wish, aren't I?*

I was slightly surprised when the screen came live, but gratified. This would, of course, go well.

'If this is about— It is, isn't it? I recognise the look on your face, Gragg.'

'Yes, but—' He was near livid.

'You're cut off, Gragg. Automatic. No more links here. *I* don't want to know. The *government* doesn't want to know. No-one does. Deal with it. Goodb—' He cut himself off mid-word.

'That went well, dad,' Cygmund had come to join us. Cedrica by his side. Holding hands. Twins do that kind of thing, so they tell me.

'Mm, didn't it just.' Yesss, it had been so predictable. 'Now, my little ones, I have total permission to whatever I want with our little find. And Regional Control doesn't want to know – you heard him. And that's recorded.' I

122

treated them to a big smile – a slightly weak one, anyway. 'We can do what we want with it. Arsy said so, didn't he?'

'We can anyway – we always do.'

'I have a feeling about this one. We've not had anything with any vestige of power lingering in it before.' I was quietly rather pleased; that slight feeling you've pulled something over on someone. 'He's got no comeback, whatever it is.'

'Yeah, right, Dad.'

'Oh, Faithless Ones,' I chastised them. 'Let's get over there and get that thing open. I reckon the double edging we exposed is the jamb around an entrance... portal... something. We need to lift it and straighten it up. With all the lectro and mech gear we have parked around, it shouldn't be too hard to open it up. And don't tell your mother.'

'Dad, you know she already knows. She always does.'

We soon had it lifted out of its hole, sitting there level and quite splendid, really. 'Nobody's ever found any of the wartime remains with integral power before. Not ours or the Yerricks.'

'Dad, it's so common.'

'Now, it is, yes. Two centuries ago, this was pioneering stuff. So. Are we going to get it open and see what's in there?

Under an hour, and it hissed. There was a quiet click, and the oval space proved it was a door, and it eased open a hand's width.

'Who wants the honour?' I invited. Yes, I know, anyone else would have made their beloved progeny stand well back. But I'm not like that. Anything to be rid of them. No, not really, but I was pretty sure there wouldn't be anything deadly in it, and they'd love being first in.

The twins did it. Very nifty on their feet, they are. Not too good at opening big heavy doors, though. Ginita had to help. 'What is it, Dad?'

I peered in over their heads. It looked so much like they're supposed to that I was surprised. A row of four incubators. Each with a body. Small. Cryogenic capsules. Exactly like they always depict them.

We squeezed into the podule.

'I never realised they were so small, for all the bother they were.' To see them in the flesh. 'They're a mite emaciated and pale, but that's living flesh you're looking at.' First time I'd seen them for real, and I wasn't at all sure they were still alive – could be dead as Mati Halott until we check them.

'Come on, then, let's have a proper look.'

We peered and poked and looked at intact dials. All the indications were that these Yerricks were indeed alive, even if very deeply cryo'd. 'Norging good technology.'

'What you going to do, Dad?'

'Tell you later. Something to check... man to see.'

I've been selling all this stuff to the yippies for three years – all kinds of relics. Anything small and preferably recognisable. There's some demand for it among our lot; and a good demand among the Yerricks themselves. It's not smuggling, exactly, not these days with relations restarted and improving. In fact, I regard myself as a peacemaker between us – selling war mementoes to the former enemy. Funny, that. But that's how it seems to work. Like they regard it as honourable ancient history – too far removed from surviving descendants on either side. Or maybe the return of heroic objects that are part of the soul of Yerrick.

The yippies make good go-betweens, and I have huge stores of relic-items. I even collect them from other plot-holders secretly. Memorabilia from the War Times – goes down well with the Yerricks.

'These are ultimate relics, Dad, actual Yerricks.' Yolanya had her head screwed-on the right way round; sees the value in everything. I taught them well.

'Are you going to turn them off and let them die? Sell their bodies?'

'Ahh, my children, I brought you up so well, didn't I? Always go for the profit item, isn't that my maxim? Sell the bodies? Let's call that option Plan B, hmm?'

'So, what's Plan A, Dad?'

What an opportunity! They are the best publicity we could hope for – two-hundred-year-old living heroes being returned home with all honours. *Living ones*. I could even sell the cryo podule as their "home" for the past two centuries. Through the yippies, I can quietly sell their management rights to a Yerrick contact I know of. I heard he's a publicity genius – he's the rep for Meritrinya Artworks, hmm? You must know them? And Sirene Sounds? Yes, he runs their campaigns. So I'm sure he can alert and capture half the universe's attention to living war heroes from two centuries back. Ha! That fool TD RC – no claim on them at all. They're mine.

'Think of the demand for memorabilia that will be created. And the resulting price boom,' I told my offspring. 'Just wait till it's all in place and working before you tell your mother, hmm?'

'Are we set, then? Wake them up? Bring them round?'

'Revive them?'

'Bring them back to life?

With all the buttons and knobs set as we thought they should be, I finger-tipped the button with not so much as a hesitation or prayer to Moneta, my Cash-God. And we sat back and waited. And shuffled round. And made a drink. And tapped the dials. And sat back again and waited.

'There's definitely something happening, Dad,' Maykti whispered, as though it would disturb them to hear outside sounds.

'I think the one on this end is looking a bit healthier-coloured.'

'Is indigo a healthy colour for them?'

We peered and whispered – that's catching, this whispering thing – and re-checked all the dials. Didn't adjust anything.

'It looks like the system does them one at a time, Dad. It's just this one so far.'

'Okay, it's definitely doing something. Think how long it takes you to wake up after one night's kip, never mind seven thousand nights.'

'It won't be wanting breakfast will it, Dad?'

Norgs! I hadn't thought of that. 'Your mother'll have something in,' I assured them. 'Hello. Look. It just moved. Twitched.'

This was norging exciting stuff. The first-ever alien revival – not that they looked all that dissimilar to us – funny colour, kid-sized, longer arms and the eye sockets looked to be bigger than ours; but their eyes were shut, so we couldn't tell what they looked like.

'Yes! Yes. Dad. It's trying to sit up.'

Cygmund and Cedrica were in there as well, helping, chattering, overwhelming the poor thing with so much audio and visual stimulation. It probably had a bit of an olfactory overload, too, after all the digging we'd been doing.

'Gently,' I cautioned them. 'It's going to be bewildered. Give it time… see, it's opening its eyes.'

Glitter-eyes as big and black as Size 9 bolt-holes. It was looking round, slowly. Realisation coming to it. I took a step forwards; the twins took one back.

'We should have had a drink ready to offer it,' Yolanya was saying.

'I expect it wants to know the score first,' I said.

'What score? Does it follow the Redball Games, do you think?'

'Why? Is it a Ghas Rovers fan?'

My kids do it on purpose. 'The score,' I told them, 'just means everything that's been happening; where they are; the passage of time; what's going to happen to them.'

It was speaking, a bit falteringly at first, but we'd had a memocryst in Yerrick, so we had the basics for communicating with it. It sounded a bit gear-box crunchy, but, well… *Its vocal cords are stiff,* I thought, and you forget words, so it'll improve, and I started to tell it what was happening, about their cryogenic podule being found virtually intact. It was looking round, like it was remembering… and realising.

127

I spoke more with it; and the kids did, too, saying it had a second chance at life. 'You can all go home, back to Yerrick as heroes of the old wars.'

'You'll be famous celebrities,' I worked on him. 'Famous and rich.' I didn't mention the huge profit I was in line for. He – I think it was a "he" – didn't need to have his mind cluttered with mundane things of that nature.

'What?' He said. 'Go back to Yerrick? To the home planet?' He looked so baffled, shaking his head. 'No... No! Definitely not. We can't go back there. We were convicts. The last thing we are is heroes...'

He was trying to get up, but I put a hand out to stop him, 'You're not strong enough yet to stand. Just rest and take it all in.'

'No, no. We're under a death sentence. On a suicide mission. Our leaders – and everyone else – hold grudges; debts and judgements last in perpetuity – they don't lapse after a couple of centuries. They'd confirm the original sentences for us and carry them out as soon as we landed. We'd be dead in a week – dismembered.

'We're damn-well not going back to Yerrick. Never. No way.' The look on his face! So determined – absolutely set firm.

Ginita leaned a bit closer, and muttered, 'I think we might be back to Plan B, Dad.'

*** PLAN B ***

128

RETIRE? ME?

Don't want to retire. Don't ever want to. The thought is terrible. What would I and The Big Vac do without each other? 'I been at this job two hundred years,' I told them. 'And I've seen a lot of changes – kept up with all the developments.'

'It's the law, Toiler,' they insisted.

'Come on, let me just move away and I'll restart afresh.' I knew it wouldn't work – they have tabs on you everywhere from Andromeda to Zylon. I've moved homes and jobs and had complete restarts before. Mutual agreement divorces. Nothing's fixed and forever. It's all flexible. And somebody keeps tabs on you.

'Yeah, it's all flexible,' the guys in the office told me, 'except retirement. You got to go.'

'Pack up.'

I knew it was coming, and was pretty much resigned to its inevitability. Talked it all over with my present family – Isobeq and the four skids. Okay, we'd retire on Parinis, and we'd be well-off, relatively speaking, with all my savings and investments. Lot of developments in two hundred years, and I had a future-investment eye on some of the newly-promising ones.

'It's the Space Working Union's fault,' I told Isobeq. 'They insist that spacers get too, well, er, spaced out, after spending that long in ships that leak air out and radiation in. But it don't get everybody like that – look at me: I'm fine, aren't I?'

I most likely shouldn't have asked, judging by the look on her face. I've probably been in four hundred

129

different ships, counting trips that only lasted a few dodecs, and up to my longest of eighteen years aboard the Wild Cat. I kept getting promoted by accident – accidents to the folks above me. Till I found myself as captain of the WC.

'I did okay at captaining, didn't I?' I tried a bit of back-door persuasion when I waylaid CE Yüce at a conference for has-beens – or Pre-Retirees, as they politely called us. 'I turned in a profit, didn't I?' That's the main thing, apart from not losing the ship, officers and crew – who, fortunately, I was able to replace at no expense to the company. They liked that. But I preferred my old job of Top Hand – i/c of all the operations, making sure everything worked, people, schedules and equipment. It all depended on which kind of oil or grease you applied to each situation.

'The answer's still No, Toiler. You got to go.'

She'd been a vitch for the past one-fifty years. She wasn't going to change now, I suppose.

After my time as captain, I went back to Hold and Handing duties as soon as I could, but they wouldn't let me move down within their company, so I left Mines JI and started back with EverStar, with whom I shared a chequered history. But we forgave each other and I went back in as Top Hand of a new Midweight Freighter, the Gettit There Star. That was better than being Captain – all I did as Captain was point it in the desired direction, but as Top Hand, I managed the ship in detail; I knew every system, how to fit'em, fix'em and get the best out of'em. Same with the crew.

And I was still on the Star as Top Hand when we called in at some Pick-up Planet whose name didn't matter to us non-exec crew. Not as if we did the buying and selling and planning routes – they had accountants and navigators for that.

Yes, we got there, alright, but the Star didn't get me back. The officer idiots were having big problems with locals, who were accusing us of trying to export some contraband. Our ship was impounded; all crew and officers held hostage as security. By the time we were released, my own union had withdrawn my Vac Worthiness card. 'You're retired as from now, Toiler. It's Official. Your card's cancelled. You're not allowed in space again.'

'How'm I supposed to get home? Wife? Family? Fortune? – relatively speaking. We're less than seven dodecs away from Parinis, just eighty days. I can go over the age by that much, surely?

'No. You're grounded. Suborbital only.'

'So I'm stuck on Dump?'

The local rep bristled. 'Laimar. Not Dump. Say it again and you'll have your atmospheric licence cancelled, too.'

Thus. Here I am. Destitute. Disenfranchised from everything. I begged to send a message carrier to Isobeq and the skids. That was a dozen dodecs back. Even by carrier, there should have been a reply by now.

But nothing. I'm dumped on Dump. When you're argumentative and out of favour, your messies home don't get far. And they're on the lookout for stowaways at the Kildon Terminal – and it's automatic airlocking for stowaways. So I'm not doing that – I've seen it a few times.

But, tell you truth, half a year on Dump – er, Garden Planet of Parinis – have not been as deadly as I imagined.

Slightly, because it's not a total pit; but mostly, because I decided to ingratiate myself, cooperate and look for opportunities to de-planet quietly.

So I had three dodecs physically handling baggage and looking for legit chances to bribe my way somewhere. Then Union Vile came sneering past one Thonday, 'Guess it's you who's dumped, Toiler. This job in baggage handling not suit you? No opportunities to cadge your way aboard anything?' Him, my nemesis, Union Mr Vile. 'I don't do the Union stuff so much now. I'm on the Board for the Company. So you stand no chance of anything without me.' I'd have gone for his throat, but I had my hands full of somebody's Balls of Hagan – the light sphere things from Hagan that are all the rage this year, apparently. His back was filled with hate-arrows before he'd gone ten paces.

He stopped, came back to me. 'You don't like handling baggage? Want to get aloft again?'

He was being stupid. *If he tells me I could have been in the Vac these past three dodecs, I'm more than ready to turn him inside-out.* 'No, not into orbit. Atmospheric stuff. We're getting a pair of new sub-orbital ships in soon. Very soon. They're supposed to be with delivery crew, handlers and captains.'

'So?'

'I heard you were up there, Top Hand?'

'Vac craft, not down here in the murk.'

'Very similar design. I gather they could use someone with wide experience. Like you? Want to have a look? See what you think?

'Yo yo…' I thought about it. Mostly about how much I despised him, and detested baggage, and loathed the hostel, and hated having the same ground under my feet day up, day down – thirty-seven consecutive days in one place is my unwanted record. 'Okay,' I said, ninety percent grudging and convinced it'd be utter betrayal of every belief I ever had in the virtue of vengeance. 'Let me take a first look.'

It wasn't bad at all. I've been in smaller full vaccers and orbiters. And they're new. I'd be the first Top Hand on the Number One Vessel, pretty much get it up and working how I wanted. 'The new crews'll need training up. All the wires and keys – they're raw hands; we want to use local personnel. Think you can do that?

'I'll look inside.'

Hmm... some systems were familiar. Orbital launch motors are the same as these, almost identical. The dials even go up to over five hundred kk, which is easily into orbit for a craft of this size and power. 'Kipps – some of these linkages won't work right,' I poked round. 'The hold's not set up properly for the mixed goods and semi-bulk stuff you're envisaging. The fuel tanks need enlarging.'

Superior, smirking yipper. He knew he had me. How I was supposed to resist an offer like this? So I took it. And did okay – four dodecs to get both ships flying with an On-Captain each. I was officially Top Hand on one of them, but I was more like TroubleGuy for both ships, travelling all round the planet. Into orbit twice. What glory that was! The two captains learned quick – they'd had the memocrysts and knew the basics, plus an update on these two we were flying.

I was just adoring it – all the plotting and planning to steal one and get back home. But, till the opportunity arose – like the limiters coming off the drives – I actually did love the sub-orbital and occasional Full-Orbit forays.

133

And just being in a job I could do right, and not many others could, certainly not on Laimar – I thought I ought to stop calling it Dump if was stuck here.

'We're expanding. Into passengers. Another two ships.'

'So?'

'You want to be captain?'

'At my age?'

And that was where Union-cum-Company Vile dropped his clanger – appointing me as captain. Captains have open permits. It's an honorary thing, but it's real, too. I'm fully cleared for atmospheric, close-orbit and full space. Submarine, too, though that wasn't going to affect me, especially not on Dump – there's not too much real sea or ocean.

I studied the plazpap he handed me. "Captain Imperial… of the seaways, airways and spaceways." Sure, it was basically a titular thing, but it was there, in purple, gold and white. Genuine and literal. That Vile thing couldn't stop me leaving Dump now I had my vac licence back.

'Sure I can't stop you. What'll you do? Steal a ship? You got more sense than to stow away. But can you afford it? Find a captain who'll take you? A hold-hand you can bribe? Get on as basic-hand? Anyway, why would you go? Where? You have things going well here. You have a home, of sorts, by the river.'

'I got a real home, back home, with my wife and the skids. I message every dodec – somebody's blocking them; must be.' I threw him my best disgusted look. 'Am I cholled-off? Yes, I cholling am. On my own half a damn year – Laimar time.'

'And another anyway… what would you say to your family in passing?'

'Eh?' That rocked my tappets. 'Isobeq? My skids? What about'em?'

'They're due here in around a dodec. I, er, intercepted your eMesses. Redirected them. Re-sent them. She's sorted things out; liquidised things back home – your four children are looking forward to a new start. Well, I expect she'll tell you when she arrives.

'You needn't look at me like that, Toiler. You won't get the chance. I run the Cotter fleet for the Company,' he said. 'There'll be four captains, with you as senior. And when I retire – which will be when we're both happy with the fleet's running – I'll give you time to learn my job. We could put Maigan in charge of the Daisy May. You'd be running the fleet – and that can be as hands-on as you want. So… suppose you use this next dodec to clean your house up, meet the fleet owners for a chat, think of anything else?

'Vile? Why… why me?'

The turdface was totally blank. 'How else was I going to get a Top Hand with your experience? We started looking for a top spacer who could do anything, around three years ago, when we were proposing and planning our atmos fleet… moving on to orbital… and then starting with our own interstellar vessels – four to start.

You can be Co-ordinator, Commander, Commodore, call yourself what you like. Sort your own role out however you wish. Hands-on-and-in-there, or distant overwatch. Orbit… whatever. Give us a year, and you can leave Laimar with everything you have accumulated, and we'll re-date your retirement licence.'

135

'You bastard. You set me up for this from the start?' My right fist caught him beautifully on his cheek, blood from mouth and nose instantly. He went down like a fart at a funeral. Twitching. A couple of his underlings were heading for me.

'Okay,' I told him. 'If my wife's willing, of course I'll do it.' Jeeps, not half. Full captain… Commodore? New fleet? That's more like how retirement should be. I stood over him, raging and rapturous at the same time.

'Just don't try standing up till I'm out the room.'

TAZZA'S A MUG

Twenty-second day of Aroga, was a particularly average, no-prospect, day, and I must have been especially introspective, too, when B-Bo came to me. 'You're Tazza?'

I looked at him with deep suspicion. Nodded slightly.

'Well, Tazza, this is your lucky day. I'm B-Bo, and I'm here with *The Plan*. I got it all worked out.'

I didn't know him from Arabin the Great, but could he talk. And he had a biggest grin and widest-open attitude I've ever come across. So I was doubly suspicious. Maybe triply.

Basically, I suppose, I go for the easiest path and hope things aren't too much bother. 'You're a mug, Tazza.' They tell me. 'It's like you've got a handle to jerk you around with.'

My excuse is that it's my mother-imposed conscience. The times I had a clout round the ear to reinforce one message or another. 'It's selfish to do things for yourself... You should help other people...' *Clout.* 'Remember that. Always.' *Clout.* 'It's called being altruistic.' *Clout.* I'm conditioned more than her hair ever was.

I make what I can of that burden, and drear my life along pretending I'm altruistic. Altruistic – Huh. That's what mum used to say. I think it means doing things without expecting any reward.

'But I do expect,' I told her. 'If I'm doing all this to help everybody else, I expect some recognition; I expect people I've helped to be nice to me; to think well of me; not take advantage of me.'

She usually slapped me when I said things like that, so I only said them to myself afterwards. I mean, it's no more selfish than the ancient prayer about not seeking any reward other than feeling smug for doing what your god wants.

'A bit of gratitude and appreciation is a small enough price to pay for all I give away,' I complained to Alexia, my moan-mate down the Slug and Solstice. 'Not that I get a twelfth of what I deserve.'

'You sound just like your mother. But, yeah, you're a mug, alright.' She didn't have to agree quite so readily, and push her empty glass my way. 'You getting me another? Tazz?'

So now, I'm sitting in my Work-Office, trying to figure whether I should do the Mates' Rates job for the Riverside Consortium who I can't really stand. Or have a day levelling off a terrace for the kids' adventure track across the face of the West Face of the valley. And I have this grinning feller – my age – coming practically bursting in with the offer of a lifetime. 'I have the maps,' he says, full of it. 'Sources of info, guarantees of origin, projections of profits, permits to enter the target area, and licence to explore, survey and sample. Plus warrants to begin extraction of minerals and ores, outline permission to expand initial mining operation. It's all here.'

In a lot of my situations, I've found it to be a lot less aggravation to swiftly surrender to it all and let people have their piece of me. So, on a day like this, yeah, I'm cholled off enough to at least give him a hearing before I swing him out. So much easier than having an instant confrontation and stirring everyone up – like all my life, it's not worth the effort of trying to fight my way to the top. I quite fancy living at the top – on The Heights, but I daren't try too hard. What if I put loads of effort in, and then fail? No – I can do without that, as well as with mum's disapprobation.

Even now she's gone, I can still hear her voice over my shoulder, feel her endless disapproval. 'Do this, Tazza. Don't do that, Tazza.' So I'm not going to change and risk an ear-clout from beyond the grave.

Thus, I end up with this respected-ish life as a contractor; known in some circles for helping with kids' events... turning up at the big game... sponsoring some local initiative. It's all low key, low-life stuff, not to impress the snooties on The Heights; just to help out the workers on the flatlands and the lower slopes. Speaking literally and metaphorically, there's a lot of us down there, and they're almighty steep slopes to climb for most of us. I'm probably a lot more altruistic than mother would ever believe – and I'd still receive a slapping for not doing more.

I know what all this stuff of B-Bo's means: it's my area of expertise. I know the ores and minerals surveying scene, and I'm very familiar with the equipment needed to do this. There's no such thing as a standard package, but if there was, this would be very typical; and it all looked genuine. I know these things, and it *was* genuine. Purely so he couldn't say I didn't give him a chance, I ran every check on the sources and likelihoods – I know which DBs to access on the hub.

I made it about half way up those slippery slopes, but never had a strong yen to leave the folk I grew up with. Besides, I like them. I do; I actually like the rougher, lower side of town… life. 'It's where you belong.' Mum said that. Often.

No – who am I kidding? That was probably mum talking. *Yes, right, I'm kidding everybody, including myself.* I could maybe scramble up the rest of the way to The Heights if I dedicated myself to it, and dropped everything else. I sometimes look up the valley slopes, and see the amazing homes on the rim – a string of them, anything from glass super-tech towers to repro legend-castles. And I sigh and sometimes wish. But I know I'd scuttle round and keep my head down if I was up there; keep looking down the slopes and wishing I was back with my own people. I wouldn't soar, like the folk already there seem to do, the ones who are born to it.

I see all the difficulties my old haunts are going through. Half of it's their own profligate fault, but I just feel obliged to help. Yeah, that costs me, but it's cheaper on my nerves than having mum ranting in my ear. So they like me, sort of. 'You? Living up there? It'll never happen,' Mum used to say, 'You belong here.'

I remember an especially hard clout to reinforce that message.

What Laughing Boy had here might just be a way up? *Don't be naïve. You're getting desperate,* I told myself, *to even glance through this lot, much less consider it.*

'Tazza,' he was persuading me, 'you have all the equipment in your contracts yard – sky-eyes, diggers, drills, two transports, analysers, porto-smelters, shelters and stores. And five years' experience. This's for exactly the type of contractor you are – heavy, industrial, mining, surveying, transporting. This is spot-on right for you,

Tazza. See? Tazz?' He was on excessive friend-terms with me already.

'So how're you seeing this?' I said. 'You provide the documentaries, and I provide the equipment. You consider that to be an equal partnership?'

'Yes. I'm being most reasonable,' he told me.

I looked over his stuff again, very closely. And he looked over mine the same. 'All your gear is rough, heavy duty, old and not worth as much as my plans.'

'Ha, but you could have prepared all this lot on-screen in a couple of days, for all the deeper checking I'd be able to do.'

But, he seemed genuine, I liked him and he was keen. I had no major works on at the time, and the crew could manage anything that turned up. And, as I said, I was feeling a tad introspective, like re-evaluating my fortunes and having a vaguely-wishing spell. And it was maybe-intriguing. So we went to the Development Office about registering the partnership.

'Sureties? Guarantees?' The Registrar asked.

'I hadn't thought it necessary,' I said. 'We're not risking a lot – wear and tear on my equipment, balanced by B-Bo's time and expenses amassing the—'

'You don't know each other.' Reggy stopped me. 'We can't sanction the matter; what if you go bust? It would leave Madry Island littered with abandoned works and spoil heaps. The Gov would clear it up at the expense of your sureties. That's DevOffice Standard. You know that, Tazza.'

I considered dropping out – didn't want unlimited risk on my home – huh, such as it was, plus my shuttle ship, savings. 'Well, it's a lot to—'

But B-Bo was agreeing straight away, 'I'll put up my house. I'm totally convinced by my sources, samples and projections.'

'That'll do it,' Reggy said. 'You, too, Tazza? That guarantees the after-contract clearance on Madry. And if one of you reneges, the other would similarly have recompense through the other's guarantee surety. "Renege" was defined as, "Desert, abandon, commit suicide, act in bad faith, provide false collateral before or after the fact..."'

'So I had to put my place and business gear up, as well as B-Bo putting his house up, as joint indemnity for the enterprise.' I felt really stupid telling Alexia about it.

'He saw you coming, Tazz. It's you all over.'

We travelled out to Madry Island, well to the other side of Piperry, 17,000kt from Base. Entirely at my expense. B-Bo wasn't much use with helping to set it up, either. But we got started on locating the mapped-out ore veins and initial test drilling within the day.

Madry Island was a rough, barren rocky place, mostly a plateau that was high in the sky – thin air, some vicious reptiles, snakes, carib insects, and scorching wind most days. 'We're lucky so far,' B-Bo tells me. 'It turns sub-zee at night.' We upped the shelter in a bare-rock gully with sensors and auto-kills on.

Once settled, we were out every day, surveying, comparing, test-drilling, sampling, analysing.

The whole thing was poor from the start... very little found. 'B-Bo, none of it's living up to your surveys on richness or locations. The ground's harder in terms of rock type and density; there's too much overburden; the terrain's too steep...'

We rocked and rolled and struggled and found thin veins of caiterite and mallinium. 'They're not even the major ores on the surveys, B-Bo.' He'd walked off by then, real jaunty, like he knew already. And I hated him for his attitude more than anything.

My main drill went down – literally – it drilled a hole thirty yar deep for the explosive, and jammed solid. Overheated. The vapour analysis showed miterium – which'll melt and re-solidify around the drill head, and wasn't on any of the lists for this area. So I lost that drillhead and a section of drill shaft; and the motor needed a full refurb, which took me three days. And it meant re-locating our survey site yet again.

'Scruggle me, Tazza,' I told myself, 'This is the muggiest thing you ever done. Alexia'll never let me off this hook if she finds out.'

Sixty days into the year-long bond, and it was time for a major review. 'I know the stuff's here,' B-Bo kept telling me over a jug of Joo-juice at the latest failed drillhead-spot. 'I *know* it.'

But the way he said it, he had no idea. That tone of voice meant, 'I *hope* there's something here.'

'We've been sending samples in for assay every octo... Young Zeke my yard lad has been semi-refining it all and taking it to the Assay Office. We've been getting scruggawful results – Zilcho percent, and the wrong metals, anyway.'

End of my temper, I heard mother's words jabbing at me, 'Always be charitable… Give the benefit of the doubt…' So I didn't strangle him, and tried to be reasonable. I fetched the maps and the survey results, the percentage assays. 'Okay, B-Bo, which parts did you invent?'

'The maps are dead straight,' he protested.

'They're not – they haven't even got some of the rivers, hills and outcrops in the right place. Who guessed at all this? Or trace-copied it off a screen somewhere?' I couldn't believe I'd been such a mug. Even me. Blinded by my need for a winner, I expect. 'What are you doing to me, B-Bo? You just know a mug a kt away, do you? And like a laugh? This's a load of lort, and you know it.'

We discussed, or *argued*, as some might say. 'So these ore and mineral surveys,' I concluded, 'are absolute inventions with fake certifications and signatures. Jipps, B-Bo, they looked utterly genuine when you brought them to me. They had all the right readouts.'

'I'm pretty good at that kind of thing,' he admitted. 'I was positive there was Hjeridium there—'

'*Hjeridium?* For Fruggsake. What gave you that idea?' This was getting worse.

'A hunch – I was reading about it, and I thought how great it would be… and this territory is just the sort of place… and the adventure…'

'So there's nothing here?'

He shrugged, 'I'm being honest with you now, Tazz—' That huge wide – forgive-me-I'm-a-little-boy – grin. I could have happily shoved a six-eight drill head through his face, but I'm Tazza, professional mug. I have a lifetime on this end of the lort-stick. I know my place, alright – it's where mother put me every chance she got.

'It's the truth *Now?* So none of this so far is true, or real? All a lie?'

He was nodding, rather molishly.

'B-Bo,' I said with infinite patience that had just collapsed all around me. 'You've conned me out here; at huge expense; and time wasted: and in poor faith – didn't you read the contract? This counts as reneging on the partnership.'

'Ah. No. It doesn't. It makes it a False Contract. Cancelled, as though never entered into.'

That took me back a bit. 'Are you mad, B-Bo? It means a contract entered into under false pretences. It doesn't negate the contract – it wipes you off it. Everything you put in is negated.'

'You've just been telling me I've put nothing in. All this is fake. So it's not a lot to negate, is it?' He seemed perfectly happy and confident about it.

'You great lort-bag.' I was lost for words. 'B-Bo, I liked you. Trusted you. How could you? We've been mates, partners. The sureties we put up; they were for just this kind of situation. Your home—'

'Ahh. That's another thing. I withdrew it.'

'You can't do that.'

'I did. Showed them your agreement and the latest assay figures I sent in – I sort of faked very rich profits – so we didn't need the surety any longer. They pulled a few fingers and faces, but that was it. I lose nothing.' He was grinning. Triumph.

'Why? B-Bo, why?'

'To see if I could. They'll do a trivid for the Rat Show if this works out. I wear a bodycam all the time. It's a great story. Scruggles – the look on your face.' Huge, totally relaxed grin.

I would have let the floor swallow me up, except mother would be down there, ready to blame me for something.

'And, you can't kill me – that would forfeit your surety, and you'd lose your house and equipment – that neat little shuttle.'

He wandered off, chuckling. We'd been working together… eaten together… laughed… got drunk. *How could he? For some ratty trivid show?*

Just one thing didn't quite ring true – I've seen him naked, showering, pre-bed, swimming; and there was never any sign of a camera. Nor anywhere among his equipment – he'd brought so little of it. And no drones hovering with long lenses. So I didn't believe the bodycam coverage bit.

And… and… would Dev Office really let him have the surety back without a genuine face-to-face meeting over it? With both of us? Probably – we'd all accepted how genuine his papwork was. 'Your house a fake, too?' I shouted after him. *Scruggit, I thought the deeds looked just as real as the surveys. Yeah, exactly. Well, whether you'd cancelled them or not, it wouldn't make any difference if they were fake anyway.*

I watched him pottering round, starting to get some things together. 'You going to run out on me already?'

'Of course,' he was laughing. 'Played you all the way, Tazza.

He left; he really did. A potbelly drone homed in on him around noon the following day – after a silent, dead night when I was sorely tempted to strangle him.

'Not even had the guts to slit my throat, eh? Or drive the dumper over me?' He mocked. One sickeningly cheerful wave, an even more gruesome smile, and he'd gone. 'See you on the trivids.'

It took me four days – listening to a ghostly-voiced mother snapping at my heels – to finish off the on-going operations. You have to allow the sequences to finish. Can't just stop them and extract the feeders and heads, drain off the analytic tubs; all that kind of thing. They're non-interruptible processes.

Then another four days to get all the equipment and gear together, cleaned off, packed up and loaded up. Then four more to piece-meal it back to my depot at Base.

There was some checkover work waiting for me on an old contract out by Comber's, and that took my mind off these four-score wasted days on Madry. Young Zeke said he'd clean out the tubs and bins, zero the calibrations and reset them, overhaul the motors. He was more thorough at it than I was. I'd trained him better than I had myself. 'You clean and maintain anything that comes in the yard,

Young Zeke, and you got a job for life – or as long as your Aunty Moyet says so.'

So when I was done at Comber's, I called in at the Development Office on the way back. 'Is there anything of mine left? Anything I can reclaim? The papwork on my surety? My house and gear and everything? Is any of it still mine?'

'Eh?' the Assistant Registrar woman said. 'Eh?' And brought out the relevant docs. All mine were returned to me, still sealed and certified. I had no idea it would be that much of a relief: I must have been deep-afraid inside that B-Bo had conned everything off me.

'And there's these of the other party's surety.' She pulled a small plas wallet out the pack; turned it over. 'His property.'

Now I was really confused. 'Me? Why? It's all cancelled, isn't it?'

Now DevOffice Lady looked puzzled, 'No. It couldn't be cancelled. It's our impression… understanding –' She dragged some pages up on screen, '– that B-Bo created all the documents purely in order to set up a false partnership with you. We had a notification to that effect, about one hour before the report of his suicide.'

'His *what?* When? How?'

The DevOffice Lady didn't need to check, 'A score and a half days back? He crashed the potbelly into a mountainside near Triap Peaks – on the return from your development claim. There was an e-blip from him a few minutes prior to the impact. Deliberate, no doubt of it.'

'So now?'

She shrugged one shoulder. 'Whatever you wish. Your partnership was dissolved on his death, and also by his admission of falsifying the papwork that was the basis of the original contract.' She glanced again through the screen info and the pap-docs, and nodded to confirm her own words.

'He cancelled his surety – his house. He told me.'

'No. He couldn't do that. It's all here.' She proffered a package. 'It's all here. It isn't his now, though – it's yours. I gather it's up on The Heights. He defaulted on several counts of deliberate malfeasance. The whole contract is nulled. I understand from the sat-pics you have left the site clean, but still have four-fifths of your option-time left. So we'll keep your surety until that time is up – just in case you decide to go back, hmm?'

'Why would I go back to a barren waste like that?'

'Oh. I thought there was a progress report a score back. Er, yes, here. From your Yard Base. Signed YL Young Zeke. Readings on Ullium and Fetrotite were high, as I recall. Let's see... Er, yes. Here... Point four on the Ullium, and point three on the other. Both exceptionally high concentrations. Keeping the secret so you can bag up the surrounding claims, are you? Be worth a fair shek.'

'Young Zeke? My yard lad?' I skipped through his report, 'He analysed the cleanings? Registered them. Fruggerty, I did train him well.'

In something of a daze, I thought I might as well call in at the supposed house I had been granted. It was on my way back to my yard base, and, 'I might as well make a long day longer.'

I circled up and around to locate the place, twice re-entering the ID codes for the location. Not often I'd taken my shuttle up there. B-Bo's home occupied the top of a knoll overlooking the town to the north, and the mountains to the south. All-round terracing. I circled round again, checking the code address yet again, and brought her down on the skypad. Right up on The Heights. 'This's a bit of a stopper,' I looked around in unmitigated disbelief. 'Lort.'

Wife and three kids. Came out to see me. That was a stopper, too.

And *so* attractive Mrs B-Bo was, too. Petite, long, dark, straight hair. Neat young…ish lady.

'Ah, Mr Savanto, at last.' She was smiling. Scruggit, I *love* freckles. 'Of course I know who you are; you're Tazza. And why you're here.'

'You do?'

'Of course, I'm not at all surprised that you're here. Upset? No, I've been expecting you; you're my saviour.'

She was Ty'eeta, and, even at first sight, she was exactly what mother would have most severely disapproved of. So, in a flash of freedom – she was triply attractive.

Beautiful place – pineya trees, rosetta gardens, pool, white walls and ochre-sheet roof. Ty'eeta insisted I go inside, for a cool C'maya Orange drink. The kids were delightful. Quiet and polite with knowing laughs. She was a revelation – calm, not bitter at all.

She's going to poison you, any moment now.

Shut up, mother.

Tazza! Don't you dare speak to me in that manner.

My mind turned to her in cold flame; my hands found the throat that gave birth to all her scathings, and my fingers tightened… tighter… not another word would I hear from that scrawky mouth. A few deft shakes, as with

150

wringing out a soddened tayola, and she was fading from my grasp and my sight...

Other eyes were there, bright and sparkling, 'Silly,' she called me. 'Haven't you figured it yet? B-Bo's time was very limited; he had cancratic growths in his brain. We talked about the future, what we would be most comfortable with, and decided to make the right provision. And spent some time looking around for the type of person I would most like to share this house with after his demise.

'And not only the type of person – the actual person. All round town, the people we see and mix with... Well, we heard about you – among many other, er, candidates. We chose you. I thought you were rather practical, funny, adventurous – and just my kind of person. And you're generous with people, quite easy-going, unwed and unattached—'

'Okay, okay. Right. You don't need to sell me to me.'

But she must have had her little speech rehearsed, 'You're not ugly – more like rugged, lived in. "He might be just your type," B-Bo said. Check the contract: the children and I come with the house – fart and fascias, as it were. I followed you for an age, watched you. I feel as though I know you well. So here you are.'

She shrugged, half-smiled – that ultra-appealing helpless look they have – sweet-smiling, freckled women.

And I'm an absolute mug for it.

151

THE FRACTUS PROJECT

'Officers and Members...' Up on the dais in the governor's conference hall, Lord Mydie tapped his forehorns for attention, glowed a deeper shade of red into his face plates, and addressed the meeting. 'We are not here to decide on whether or not the financial support for the Inzani will be continued, or at what level. That has been decided: the Fractus Project will *not* continue. We are very much aware that this will be a blow to Moimana Sayida, manager of the Project, *but it is ended.'*

There was a general hum and glubble around the room – some people shocked, some already in the know. A tentacle or two vibrated in agreement, and one or two mandibular graspers clattered together in an about-time-too attitude.

'The Council has settled the end of the funding already,' Lord Mydie continued. 'The money allocated by Sansāra FedFund as part of the Lost Colony Revival Scheme – The Fractus Project – has come to the end of its ten-year life. In view of the near-complete failure of the project, the funding will not be renewed.'

'That financial support,' Vice Chairman Farrel ritually closed his nominal folder, 'was intended to revive the life of the Inzani after several centuries of non-breeding and near-total collapse of their culture, economy and trade contacts. If their breeding had been renewed, their society could be welcomed back into the Commonwealth. All efforts in those directions have now come to an end.'

'But they'll become extinct.' Someone protested. 'There are only a few thousand left now.'

153

'Mmm, they seem to have a self-extinction drive that has proved impossible to reverse.'

'It is the way of evolution.' A nameless official on the platform murmured; more members were in agreement with the abandonment than were against it.

Judging by the purple tinge of his platelets, VC Farrel would brook no further debate on the matter. Not that there had been a lot of debate. None, in fact: it was a financial decision, taken by the analysts, ratified by The Council.

'Indeed,' Madam Secretary PSO confirmed, 'We now decide on how rapidly we can withdraw support from this decayed colony, isolated outpost, long-lost experiment... call it what you will.

'But—' A lost voice went unheeded.

'It's a failure. We are not here to argue any further. We do *not* provide eternal subsidy; or species re-creation for a hopeless, non-self-helping society that should be allowed to die – it's the law of life. Even the much-heralded Fractus method has had no success in encouraging their breeding. Maybe this species was a mistake, an experiment by the Ruach that wasn't viable—'

'It was once – somewhere, sometime, in the Humanic Federation.' The lone voice continued its vain plea.

'Until it became a dying remnant after the Federal Collapse. Fed funds are limited. The Council is not prepared to throw its limited monies at this enterprise any longer. The Inzani have not responded in ten years.'

'But they are so *different,*' Sayida appealed, eye stalks aquiver. 'They need more time. They are fifty percent humanoid RRNA – the rest is a metalized plasmix with organic sub-crystalline nerves. Practically ageless in human terms. They are unique; hence the need to use the

154

Fractus system to grow their inner fibres and nerves in ever more complex networks. A veritable Fractus of being.'

'And that's what makes the whole project so enormously expensive to subsidise,' VC Farrell iterated. 'They continue to decline. Barely five thousand when discovered, they have declined in number since, despite all our efforts.'

'*Your* efforts have been manipulating money donated by the Fed – not involvement. Inzani reproduction is so different from that of all other humanics. They deserve so much more. We could still learn so much. They reproduce by a semi-clone growth system – based on a mix of four contributing sources. They grow full-size beings in the vats, and enhance their mentality with additions from the information banks. They then need to mature in their thought processing. They are "born" as it were, fully formed, requiring only their mind-set to be refined.'

'That's half the trouble, Moimana Sayida. They don't reproduce.'

'Yes, they do. It's just that their new-borns are full-size, and have no developed mentality.'

'Exactly, there have been no *viable* births for a decade. They seem to have no interest in perpetuating themselves. They gave up their attempts to reproduce long before now – their own incubation chambers and vats are clean, unused. There are stocks of body material. Their techniques are lost.'

'And so is their will to do anything about it.'

There was always someone who knew nothing who was prepared to back up the Lord God known as Saving Money.

'Indeed so; they are a *Non-dynamic* species,' Lord Mydie rejoined the dismissal of the protest. 'Many former Inzani beings are in storage or breakdown banks. They do nothing to help themselves. Despite the decade's investment, we have to admit that the project has been pretty much a total anti-climax. Not one successful "birth" of a new being.'

'*Please*, Sirs and M'dames, we *can't* dismiss them – forget them, not just like that. We are learning so much about the Fractus process itself, refining the mixes, the timings, the strength, the level of power inputs and the amount of intellectual information and background we feed into them before their emergence. There's too much resting on—'

'*Enough.* It is decided. Your role as Moimana – The Birth-Giver – shall cease.'

'But they are as much robot – synthetic – as Humanic. Humans created them in their own image. Such a metabolic combination is unique in the known universe, and therefore—'

'*They don't reproduce, Moimana Sayida*. They are doomed if they cannot reproduce by themselves. Sansāra Central Funding has ceased, as of now.' Vice Chairman Farrell pressed an imaginary button to emphasise the finality of the decision. 'That is the end of it.'

'May I stay on?' Sayida pushed her words in swiftly. 'I wish to try other approaches. The Humanic Historic Society – and other institutions – will fund one more year – and monitoring thereafter, as may be decided ongoingly. They attach—'

'Yes, yes, yes. We understand—'

'Thank you.' Lone Voice Sayida clapped her hands to signify the end of her arguing.

'But I meant—'

Lord Mydie was too late. Sayida, now the sole Moimana to the Inzani, had turned away. He realised he had inadvertently given his permission. *Ah well, no matter. It will continue to fail for another year at someone else's expense.*

'Sayida!' Secretary Haat's patience had worn thin. 'If you wish to stay and continue, we will not obstruct you. You may retain whatever equipment you want. All else will be wound down over the coming two deccas. Satisfied?'

Moimana Sayida smiled and turned momentarily, 'Such kindness, Madam Secretary. I have here a list of the facilities we wish to retain...'

Sayida, the Birth-Giver, surveyed the Number 4 Genetic Facility of which she had recently become Full Guardian. 'We shall change course.'

'On which aspects?' Timina, her volunteer assistant from the Humanic Historic Society was curious about whatever Sayida planned to do next.

'Firstly, Timina, your title is now Matrona, not Volunteer Eight-Six. You and I now have one year to turn this project around and make it the success I know it can be.

'A fractus is a putting-together from that which is fractured, or fragmented, to become a reborn whole. We've been creating living growth from the disparate elements of life. We have created life, but now we need to make it viable, self-aware, life. Come.' She led her assistant down the gleaming footways between the double rows of sealed vats, 'And to do that, we need a complete change of direction. We will retain these huge shiny cauldrons, and the ten days of stirring the mix of raw body materials. The same basic process of seeding with four random RRNA samples; then heating and cooling will continue – they are technically essential.'

'I've been involved in the after-process, of course,' Timina said as they looked at the enormous array of equipment that surrounded each fermentation unit, and studied the readings for the end vat. The whole place was technically very impressive – a testimony to the skill of the previous over-manager.

'And I was under-manager – basically in charge of the mixing and growth process. I succeeded in growing full-sized humanics, the new Inzani, but they had no mentality, and each had to be eliminated when our efforts at post-emergence intellectual development failed.'

'I helped to monitor them for temperatures and fluidity as the mixes began to coalesce and form a being.'

'Of course, and, whatever Lord Mydie and his crawlers-on say, the Inzani fully cooperated with all our attempts to grow these new members of their society. But,' They resumed their walk into the adjacent Mind Facility. 'But the new beings are blank-minded, despite the insertion of thinking samples from the banks. A dump of four separate, randomly-chosen thought banks was the accepted norm, so the mental RRNA would be varied. We've tried everything the Inzani suggested, remembered or dug out the banks.'

In truth, Timina wasn't sure why she'd volunteered to stay on – the lure of another year's secure funding? The possibility that the Moimana might produce a breakthrough? 'It's an area that's amazed me from the day I started as an observer. The thought that we could create life is just so awesome. I think it every time I patrol these rooms and basements. If only the mind-dumps had taken…'

'But they didn't: the fractus process is fractured somewhere along the way. For ten years, we've been creating perfect, full-sized, living beings that developed little or no mind. The Inzani have advised and supervised at every stage, so it's all exactly how they say it should be. Whatever we tried, it made no difference to their mentality. The new bodies are incapable of thinking. The Inzani have no idea what to do next: they expected to have fully-functioning newcomers, not mindless synthetic bodies waiting to be switched on, as it were. They completely reject them.'

'But you have something in mind, Moimana? A new direction, you say?'

'All this has been oriented towards *the system*… the procedures… the technical aspects of the Inzani. I'm sure we have the methodology right, down to the last syllable in the minutiae, but it doesn't work. We must be missing something. I'm going to appeal to their human half. Come. We need to empty all the vats. We're starting afresh – we will begin from the true beginning. This is the *reborn* Fractus Project. Go find the Inzani technicians, staff, sponsors. I need thirty-four volunteers.'

The gleaming metalwork was forbiddingly clean; the tall vat units scrubbed and empty. The power screens that would display the interiors, and show the data of development, were now blank and the lights dead. The Inzani stood around in semi-metallic, half-human splendour – such beauteous creatures, the nearest things to

159

the fabled ancient humans that existed. *But so unknowingly innocent after centuries of destitute isolation,* Sayida thought as she called them to order. 'Choose someone to be your partner, and hold their hand... Yes, I know it's unusual.'

'Er... My hand?'

'Yes.'

'Of course.'

'Maddo? Can you...? Thank you. And someone to be with Timina? Thank you, Korel. Now, everyone please choose a vat-unit and stand by it.'

The bewildered shuffling settled down as everyone complied, and Sayida continued. 'Right. That is your own personal vat. You are no longer a whole-facility team. We are eighteen working *pairs*. Thus, we are now called *pairents*...'

'Now...' Timina took over, standing by Vat 13. 'Please choose a colour from the spray palette... and paint a name on your vat – get rid of the number.'

'Any name. One you like? Perhaps one you make up, or heard somewhere?' Sayida smiled round in encouragement. 'Fine, it doesn't matter if you can't think of one just now, or agree on one. That can come later, as long as you have some colour and no number for now, hmm? Maybe put your own names – like Korel-Timmy?'

Looking at each other, baffled, but murmuring a host of name-like words, Sayida was pleased that her project had at last come to being, 'Er, yes, this is similar to some traditions on Sansāra Central, or Erith – my home planet. Timina?'

'Yes, on Loelei, as well.' Timina smiled at some distant memory. 'We think of names for the newcomers to our society before they arrive.'

One hour of bafflement, consternation and/or amusement saw The Vatroom transformed. 'We now call it "The Pairentage", Sayida explained. 'The storesroom at the end has been cleared-out and we have seats and cushions and games and all sorts in there – we'll call it the Hermitage. It's for we pairents. It will remain open all the time, day and night. So will the Mums'n'dadsery – it used to be called the canteen.' She still cringed at Timina's suggestion for the name, but had felt obliged to let Timina have an up-front stake in this enterprise.

'Drinks and snacks in there are free and unlimited – fix your own whenever you wish. If you want to bring in your own comfortable seating, and pictures you like to place around any of the rooms, or in The Pairentage... or the Hermitage or Mums'n'dadsery.'

She gazed around her new charges, well-pleased at their cooperation so far, 'And the whole Inzani Revival Project will henceforth be known as The Maternity Suite.

She clapped a pair of spare handicles in satisfaction at the way matters were proceeding. 'Now that we each have laid claim to a specific naissance vat for ourselves – in twosomes – we need to begin the process of creating our new beings— No no. Stay where you are. The place where you now stand is your personal birth chamber; your individual naissance. We never will say "vat" again. Each unit is now to be called your "womb".

Alright? If someone wishes to begin the infilling of the first mix? It requires both persons in each pairing to press the two buttons – yes, the blue and pink ones. Press one each. Yes, right... A little round of applause, please, while we watch the birth chamber fill up with the fractal mix.'

Ten minutes later, the chamber was filled with a fine, murky mix of minerals, metals and organics. And both

161

members of the partnership touched the pad to begin the three-decca mixing, electrifying and settling process.

'Okay, fine. Let's all move along to the next chamber. Who's is this beautiful sky-green one, called... Mirriam-Lainee, is it? How lovely.'

Within two hours, the process was completed, and the Inzani were peering at the screens and readouts for their own vat... er, naissance chamber, womb. A few compared readings, took copies, decided to keep their own personal record of changes, in addition to the log book and pads attached to each chamber.

Some stayed. Others went to the Hermitage lounge or the Mums'n'dadsery. But no-one left. They chatted in bewilderment or excitement. Whether in doubt or hope, they all chatted.

'Sayida?' Timina greeted the Moimana first thing next day. 'Three pairs stayed overnight on the lounge chairs, and checked their naissances at intervals.'

'How wonderful, and I saw several twosomes going off together last night for some hastily arranged venture; one couple even holding freshly-polished hands.'

Within two days, there was almost a routine among the Inzani of getting in early or later; together or taking turns. Some began listening in on the headphones – as though there would be anything other than slight static or faint echolalic music to hear. 'But it seems, sort of, *right*,' one pair said.

'Maybe your little naissance mixture can hear your thoughts.' But they all laughed, or smiled, or wondered, about Timina's thought. And several more duos were tuned in next day, thinking their thoughts into their womb.

Within two deccas, they were getting the idea, 'You, personally, are fully responsible for the homogeneous mass in your own naissance chamber. You've already sprayed some lovely names up there, and I've heard you talking to your naissance and each other, using those names. You've created some lovely scarlet, amber, violet or sea-pink designs, by the way.

'There will be no State Authority responsibility at any stage. We are on our own. We need to help each other. I've seen some gorgeously personalised chambers – so individually decorated. Well done, all of you.'

In four deccas, the consternation was enveloping them – the whole mass of accountability was weighing them down.

'We decided to move into the lounge area, to be close.' One couple confessed.

'We're trying to be more conscious of our own health,' two pairs confided. 'We're exercising, eating and drinking more healthily.'

'And getting plenty of sleep,' or off-switch time, as they phrased it.

Whatever else, they all turned up to check their naissance every day, even if two pairs had stopped coming for the twice-a-dec meetings for chats and talks with Sayida and Timina.

In eight deccas, they were all comparing sonagraphs, molterics, endomitros and every other analysis measure and picture it was possible to do. Each with their personal naissance mass's name on it, and not a vat number in sight.

'Isn't it amazing, the tiny differences in so many aspects?'

'Right,' Moimana Sayida brought them together in the lounge. 'We all know the key development markers and timings for our newcomers. Now we're coming to the time when we introduce a mix of four random RRNA masses into our individual mixes. Except, that's not what we're going to do this time. We will take the RRNA from only two sources. One from each of you pairents will go into your own womb mass.' She saw the puzzled looks around her. '*Growth*. The fractal elements – *your* own elements – will fuse. This will be a time of unfolding replication, of expanding topology of our *young Zani.*'

'But each is little more than a mass of liquids and gels, growing together, congealing—'

'But becoming more complex as neuron patterns begin to develop and come together. As we have been listening in to their non-thoughts, we have to remember that this is a two-way process – they listen to you – they will have become attuned to your thoughts and waves and patterns – as a familiarity of background. Although, of course, their thoughts are still almost totally undifferentiated, this is the time when we seriously begin to personalise our new people – note the word – *Personalise*. Make them a *person*. Your thoughts now will be absorbed and will begin to shape them.'

'But… a person, whether Inzani, Humanic, Dithrian or Hrypsid, is a vastly complex thing.' One of the more scuffed couples looked confused.

'Indeed so. You have a lot to do – a mass of options and preferences that we have to help them to see, to acquire, to understand. We need to think these things into them.'

'Like what to eat, drink?'

'Or what kind of work they might do?'

'Where to live… social circle…?'

'Oh, La-*roid!* Suppose he's a Hitters fan?' Miltoony and Yemma were aghast at the thought.

'Or doesn't drink?' Mack Tierphul was equally horrified.

'I absolutely can't permit mine to eat raw mye-teek seafood.'

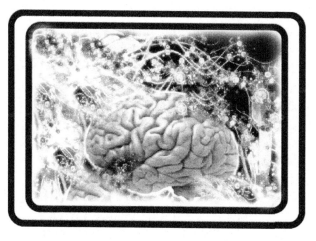

'There's a small technical problem with the naissance chambers, Timina. We need to terminate the operations of the development programme a little earlier than first thought. It simply means that our newbies will be with us sooner than we expected.'

'But Sayida, they'll be under-developed.' Timina was instantly seeing all kinds of difficulties, and half-formed creatures emerging from their chambers – her own included.

'Not if we give them more, and closer, support before and after their birthing – and being there during it. Koh?'

'You mean, it'll be up to us to guide them? To shape them?'

'We will *create* them.'

'But the lectro inputs and memo-channels?'

'We cannot depend on them; we need to *personalise* our Young Inzani, like we said – how they think. Are they empathic? Humorous? Hard-working? The direction in which they develop immediately before and after their birth is up to us – what we expose them to.

'All the previous efforts produced merely the bodies, and no awareness or intelligence. We must do whatever we can to give out newbies both of those things – and *personality*. Remember, they will be virtually full-size, physically well-developed Inzani. They need to be moulded throughout the whole process. As much now as ever in the past.'

'Wouldn't want Zorlu dressing like a Silko…'

'Or not liking poetric knowledge…'

'I think our Mitron will be bigger than us… need to make sure he knows how to behave.'

'The big decision that faces us all,' Sayida addressed the meeting, 'is, Will you want to know your newcomer? Be social together? Is your chosen name femmy or sculino? Perhaps you could give your newbie two names? One of each, or neutrals, and let them choose?'

'Yes… yes… of course. After all this time and effort; got to make sure… be there.' The thirty-four volunteer pairents were unanimous in their need to continue, and be as closely involved as possible.

166

'Are you going to want to be there at the opening of the naissance?' Timina asked.

'Yes, yes… Of course we are.' Every one of them excited that the time was upon them, worried at the suddenness of it, the responsibility.

'Remember, you will be the person they see and speak with first; go for a birra with; whose friends they will meet. You will need to do all you can to shape them, make them aware, able to continue their learning beyond their time in the womb.'

'So, now my Jezzi has RRNA from me and Aris, and is blending nicely. The fractal ingredients are complete, so we need to get tuned in with her through the headphones? Use the lectro memo feeds? Shape her development? Her thinking?

'Or his…'

'My word, Sayida, you were so positive in there. Do you really think they will emerge—'

'Be born,' Sayida corrected Timina.

'…will be born with so much knowledge and skill and awareness? Considering none in the past ten years has emer— *been born*, with more than an extremely rudimentary mentality?'

'We shall find out, shan't we? We just need to give them time to build their relationships, encourage them at every development and corner, every glitch and k-stone. They have to feel needed, and valued at every long step as their Young Zani develops under *their* influence—'

'Instead of the massed lectro banks.'

'Just so.'

'That was the day you did it, Sayida.' Timina sat back as the last of the group left.

'*We* did it, Timmy. They even call them "kids". I do, too.'

'They're all still in close contact with their pairents.' Timina looked across the Hermitage Lounge at her own newbie, chattering away with a couple of others – one a newbie, the other a Pre-Zani.

'Helped them to get jobs…'

'Or employed them directly…'

'And they all know each other…'

'Some meet up regularly…'

'One group goes to the Highball games together…' Sayida was slightly deprecating in her view of anyone who would attend such events.

'I gather two lots of them have paired up – close social. They call each other "friends".

'There's a waiting list to get onto Fractus Two – which we commence next decca with three dozen pairent couples. Five pairings are repeats from this last group, the others are new and very keen.'

'I think you started a whole social revolution here, Sayida. How'd you do it? The ideas? The answers to *everything?*'

Moimana Sayida smiled, and considered her response, eventually admitting, 'It was on Erith. I had seven children there. Young Gruud-Meredith here makes eight.' She smiled in absolute fondness at her newbie, a hand taller than her, the gleaming sheen of torganic itanium and coridium so beautiful in the soft light. A true, living, breathing, thinking Inzani Humanic.

'Merry's my first non-fully humano-organic birth, of course, but she's so lovely. On Erith, newbies are born to

168

the female of the species – with male input in the earliest stages only. They grow within the female – yes, actually inside their own body – in the primary stages, and the birth takes place early in the development process. Most of the growth takes place semi-independently afterwards, and the male partner adopts a more involved role at that stage.

I simply applied the same principle here. We used to have preparation groups, called perinatal classes. As the name implies, these take place before and after the time of the birthing, to support the pairents and their expected, or newly-arrived, family member. They call the new ones "babies", and the classes aid the newbies' chances for future conformity with standard expectations.'

'Sounds wonderful,' Timina gazed super-fondly across to her own newbie, slightly taller than she was herself, looking forward to giving birth to another in the second tranche. 'It can't have been called the Fractus Project, then?'

'Oh, no. They were called Young People's Antenatal and Recreation Classes for Encouragement and Support.' She paused, lost in nostalgia for those old times... 'The TPA... Er... the YP ARCES?'

The look on Timina's face was one of disbelief. 'You called yourselves the Wipey Arses?'

'Yes, certainly. Why not?'

'Er... Never mind.'

THE JOLLY SMALL CLUB

'I say, they're jolly small. You chappies should start a club, you know.'

Legend has it, as scribed in every edition of the Society's bi-annual publication, that these were the words spoken by Lord Harby in 1823.

'At the time,' the committee chairman told me when I applied for membership, 'he was studying the models of five architects who were vying for the design and building contract for his new stately pile. He kept the models and designed the family home himself.'

'In high dudgeon,' the society secretary continued to give out the information that all members were expected to be aware of, 'the architects conferred, sued him for the return of their models, and began the society, The Jolly Small Club.'

'And still we thrive. In keeping with the original self-imposed rules, all models must be a) a building, and b) less than a foot across.'

'Your submission,' they jointly sniffed, 'is, er, adequate to gain you membership.'

'Barely...'

'You'll improve.'

And thus I was welcomed in to The Jolly Small Club.

The original models for Lord Harby each had a glass bell jar placed over them, for protection, and to prove they were of a qualifying size. It's still a tradition that the winning entry for the annual competition is preserved within an inverted glass jar, as proof that it meets the rules. It then joins the original five on public display in the Great Hall of Lord Harby's mansion.

'I try really hard,' I was saying to the others on the committee only recently. 'I desperately want to see my name on the cup. But I'm not good enough, I know. But I keep trying.

'To see my name as the victor, practically emblazoned on the winners' board over the fireplace! T'would be such wonder, but, alas, "Peter Windlass" will never be there.'

'Indeed not,' they needlessly and very promptly agreed.

'I study the techniques of all you who have won, and I experiment with a variety of materials, but maybe I'm just not dedicated enough.'

'How true,' Dr Shipham said, rather cruelly, I thought. 'You aren't good enough.'

'Lacking in skill.' Jacob backed him up.

'And imagination.' Mr Hitchin reinforced my deficits. So nice to have friends like these – fellow committee members, anyway.

'I'm maybe fourth or fifth best, and there's only fifteen of us in the mix altogether. My best-ever was third, for a gatehouse with a barbecue party around the back porch,' I was telling our only lady member, Miz Thickra, when she first joined us. Serbian, we thought, or Swedish, but she never said – I didn't recognise any of the non-English words she occasionally let slip. 'Tiny figures or animals are allowed – in fact, they're becoming expected nowadays; it helps with displaying the scale.'

'I'm *Thyone* Thickra.' She smiled, rather weakly; uncertainly, perhaps, and said little. She continued to say little for several years, but clearly took it all in, and asked questions, but rarely answered any. In truth, her work was as stunning as she was – a smile I drowned in, and long, burnished-gold hair. I went down a ranking, to fifth or sixth best, but it almost felt like a privilege to be that close to perfection.

In her five years with us, she has won the competition the last three times. Her tiny works are utter masterpieces in every brick, stone and tile; every pane of glass and blade of grass. Each minute figure could have been a person you knew – an inch high but recognisable when you scrutinised it very closely. 'You must have the tiniest cutters and brushes, and the steadiest hand, in the whole world.' I told her, lost in admiration, as I handed her the First Prize.

She took a lot of stick – being a woman, mostly – sheer jealously on their part. By "their" I mean Jacob, Mr Hitchin, and Dr Shipham – I was at school with him, but we never got on – narky kind of man. They became worse and worse with her: snidey comments, correcting her use of English, taking the mick out of her name: Thicky, they called her… stealing her brushes and a tiny flexi razor she'd made herself.

But they took the mick outa my name, too. 'Windlass?' Jacob crowed, 'Windlass? Sounds like "Woman breaking wind".'

'Yeah, "TartFart",' Hitchin and Shipham sniggered, and went cackling off. "Tart Fart and Windy Lass…"

I liked her – she stood up to them; gave almost as good as she got, and upped her rate of perfection. This year's entry? I saw it at the Midway Meeting, where we bring our next entry in for show, and for comments on how well it's going – part of the Society scene – learning from each other. We're a Friendly Society; we constantly remind ourselves and each other of that, especially when the comments get biting, and sarcastic. But she took it well – sat with me at the finger buffet and let me buy her a drink when the provided ones all turned out to be non-alcoholic.

A shout and crash from the centre of the room. Shocked voices. Clattering and gasping. We looked. Alan Hudd the treasurer was heading our way, 'I'm sorry – a terrible accident... Your model, Miz Thickra... it's... it's...'

Destroyed. Shipham had tripped and fallen, grabbed out for support, clutched her model. It had crashed to the floor and he had landed on it. 'It looks like a flight of B17s came over on a bombing run,' said Mr Hitchin. Of course, Dr Shipham was all apology and faint smirk, and so were his two cronies.

I thought Thyone was going to have a collapse or a fit at first. But, slowly, she recovered from her near-catatonic shock and choking gasping episode, and was superbly self-controlled. She didn't attack Shipham – I would have done – and pasted Jacob and Hitchin, too, the gigglesome duo. She couldn't stop shaking, so I picked up the mass of splinters and millimetre-cube bricks. Shike! No wonder she won the last three years – no sheet walls and roofs here – she'd built them brick by microscopic tile. We carefully swept the scattered wreckage up, packed the bomb site into its carry box, and I took her home – she was in no fit state to drive.

She lived alone and let me in – I was carrying the box and pretty distraught myself. We had a drink, and she chatted – so sad and serious. 'Thyone? Unusual name?'

'It is from my home,' but she didn't expand. We talked of work and families and holidays – we shared a birthday! I felt more like I knew her – could imagine us both appearing and crying and being cleaned up and presented to our respective mums. 'No,' she said, 'mine wasn't like that. Take another drink with me. I will work with the model another day.'

I did have another drink – several – some foreign liqueurs and beers. 'I never heard of this one, Paaliaq?'

'You haven't?' she smiled and opened me another.

No no – not bed or anything like that. We talked and it was mostly me just taking an even more real liking to her. And she seemed to thaw out more than I'd seen at any of the meetings. 'Thyone,' I persisted, 'where is a name like that from?' I studied the bottle labels for clues as to their joint origin.

'Thyone? Take your pick – Greece, Mexico, Canada, India... Sheffield... Jupiter?' She had the most enigmatic smile. 'It's a moon of Jupiter – but it's too small to be my home, I'm afraid. Although the idea's nice, isn't it?'

I sat there and Googled it on my mobile phone: "One of many lovers of Zeus, mother of Dionysus..." 'Not a bad pedigree,' I told her... 'Or a star in a Frank Herbert book?' I treated her to my invitingly quizzical little-boy look. 'Or a sea cucumber?'

'Do not even think that,' she warned me. 'Stick with considering the others.'

I slept on the settee, took her back for her car next morning, and saw her for a drink and a meal at the weekend. 'I'm largely over it now,' she said when I mentioned the catastrophe. She shrugged and talked of other things as well as modelling – changing the subject whenever it veered towards her family. Her childhood didn't sound too convincing; but she was starting to become a laugh-a-minute with tales of travels and people at work.

'Yes, I would like to meet you sometimes, Peter,' she said, 'but I work away a lot. I'm not always here.'

About a month later, she announced, 'I have re-started my model for the competition. A complete recommencement, in fact. I threw the other one away.'

'What! That smart little Greek building? That model had real style and atmosphere and age.'

'I decided to recreate one of the original buildings that I have seen in the hospital grounds; it's probably accommodation for senior staff at times, or offices, clinic rooms and suchlike. I loved the style.'

'How do you get the detail?' I asked when she showed me the start she'd made. 'It's just incredible.' I marvelled at every tiny fraction of its perfection.

'Perhaps I show you one day. I have an inverse projector that surveys a building, and stores all the measurements in great detail, so I can re-create it when I project it on the base plate. It is like a hologram… a three-dimensional ghost building there. I build with that as my 3D plan.'

I left it at that, my curiosity kind of satisfied – I'd known she had to have some kind of secret method to be *that* perfect. Like, for centuries, artists have used all kinds of gadgets to get perspectives and proportions right for their masterpieces. This must be just a modern version of that.

We became friendlier. I had very few close friends, being a quiet sort of feller, and just not good in company, especially women. But I took her to a couple of pubs that were lively, and I knew some of the other drinkers to chat with.

Thyone really liked the whole thing – the scene of a comfy warm pub with atmosphere and background music… a darts and crib match in the other bar. Lots of chatter and a raffle coming round, followed by some victory singing and sandwiches.

'They have a victory song for a darts match?'

'They're very keen,' I tried to explain, wondering about the strange pastimes some people have.

'I have a small boat. You could come on it?' I offered. 'It's only small – one mast and two sails, but we could sail round the point at Dorley Ness and have a drink in the Seafarers'? Its architecture is most admirable. We could have a meal, and be back well before dark.'

You wouldn't believe the dubious look she gave me, but she came, and she loved it, even the seasick feeling. The boat, the open water, the finesse of easing alongside a jetty under sail. 'I hate to use the motor, and I'm good at close-quarter sailing. It's a matter of pride,' I said as we tied up.

The harbour at each end of our trip was a marvel to her. She'd never been at sea before, nor eaten fresh-caught seafood, or smelled the salty air… the whole seaside thing. 'What is *that?*' she gazed amazed at an old three-master, a modern repro of a schooner.

'We can have a visit around her if we come again,' I offered.

'I think I'm in love with big old ships,' she told me later. 'After the competition this year, I shall make a model ship. That one.'

But it was the Jolly Small Club's annual competition that took her time and attention for the next months, and she created the perfect model of a building. An edifice of patterned red brick, with yellow-brick diamond shapes; stonework architraves between floors, and around the windows and corners; carved gable and chimneys. A so-real tree; bushes and flowers from exactly that time of year.

The competition date loomed closer. 'I'm almost finished,' she said as she let me see her masterpiece, and I showed her my pathetic scrap of a shack. 'Just the figures to add,' she told me.

A couple of days before the Day of Judgement, as the Society referred to it, there was a rumour that Mr Hitchin had vanished from home. 'His wife's worried,' Jacob informed us at a committee meeting. 'The police have been making enquiries, but he's an adult – and married men disappear as often as single ones.' We all shrugged, as though understandingly.

Come the day, two of the expected entries were missing – Dr Shipham's and Jacob's. Jacob's mum arrived with his model just in time; it was such a shame that she let it slip as she was handing it over to Thyone. Dr Shipham's effort wasn't found until afterwards, in a locked cupboard. 'Nothing special,' was the general opinion.

Thyone's won. Of course. Every detail was perfect – someone knew the building in question, in the hospital grounds, 'I think Dr Shipham lives there. In fact, see? Doesn't that look just like him, in the entrance?'

We clustered round, filled with admiration for this piece of perfection. 'And his companions, don't they look like Hitch and Jacob?'

'How clever. So clear, so tiny.'

'So real,' we all agreed. 'It really could be them.'

'Thyone,' I asked, 'that projector of yours? Is it a bit like my computer? You know, I can "Copy" And it makes a copy of an image or a text file? Or I can do a "Move" command, and it shifts the actual image to its new place... and deletes the original?'

'What do you mean, Peter?' Such innocence in those eyes! 'You imagine that—? Ah, I see. You think my inverse projector has performed a "Copy, Move and Delete Original"?'

'Erm, well, er... just wondering. You know?'

'Best not to wonder, Peter, my love. Why don't you stay at my place tonight, hmm?'

'Er...' I was suddenly fretting about this.

'There's nothing to worry about, my Peter. Nothing for *you* to worry about. Just don't wonder about such things again, hmm, my Sweet? Nothing at all.' She hugged me – that wondrous little smile! 'Suppose you take me sailing tomorrow, hmm?'

THE POLES OF ZAY'MIÁ

I haven't been so well of late,
But it's hardly a first for any of us.
Out here on the farms of Zay'mia
We're often laid up for a time,
But get over it and back to the land.
One local bug or another, it seems,
Till we've caught the spectrum
And immuned ourselves to every one.

It's been a few days, but I manage to eat
And look out the windows and over the fields;
Down the slope, across the meadows
As far as the barns where the livestock goes
On storm-lashed nights.
So common out here
On the colony planet of Zay'mia.

The original folk, whose planet this was,
The soft and wingless hominés
Are working still; they don't need me
To tell them how, or guide their labour
As I see them digging along the hedges,
And here and there. 'Removing the roots
And the stumps of cut-down trees,' I said.

'They're not,' said Maise, who came to me
This early eve when the sun was red.
'You've gone away,' I said to her.

'I died,' she said, 'and this isn't me.
They're digging the holes where your body will go.
They'll cut you up and scatter the parts.'

'You'll guard the farm from here and there
And everywhere and all around.
Your spirit will roam the fields, like mine,
Your head on a pole at the centre point.
You'll clear the vermin and scare the thieves.
The farm'll prosper beneath your gaze
From the top of the pole in Middle Lea.'

'Ridiculous,' I waved her away.
'I'm feeling better than ever just now.'
'You may be right for one more night,' she said.
'But when they raise the totem pole,
You'd best be ready to make your peace.'
'A fantasy.' I shook my head in disbelief.
'I'm dreaming this. I see no pole out there.'

'I spoke those very words,' said Maise,
'When your father appeared and counselled me
Five years ago, that lightning night I died.
You think they dig to clear the stumps, but No:
The corner holes will take your arms.
Skirting the hedge are more for your legs.
Your chest will lie beside the stream.
Next to the shelter your stomach will rest.
These indigenes are fighting back.'

She faded then and I was alone
And cold in the darkening gloom.
She'd farmed the land that's next to mine

Till the night of the storms and lightning cracks
When the griping illness came to her.
My father before had sickened the same.

I look again from my window high.
No sign out there of a rising pole
To mount my head and glower round.
But close by the shelter they've dug a pit,
And another one down by the water's side.
Four corner holes, one arm in each?
And eight more pits along each hedge;
With room for a leg in every one.

These hominé squirls want back their lands?
No way, for I'm feeling fine, and I'm well again.
And anyway, as Maise just said, there isn't
An upright post out there to mount my head.
Though a pang of worry takes hold of me,
For down in the yard a gang of squirls
Select a post from the lumber pile,
And carry it out till it's lost in the shade.

These maggoty squirls, these hominés,
These human serfs, have lost their planet of Zay'mia.
It's too late now. Their Earth is ours.
But then again – so sharp, my pain's renewed.
Deep within, a spasm that wracks and bites.
And now I think: 'That fresh-cut log the squirls
Had held, where were they taking that pole tonight?

THE PORTAL

'This is where they must have disappeared.' Archie and I stood in the middle of the track, and looked at the circle of totally bare earth.

'Smells a bit burned, Enid.'

'Mmm,' I sniffed. 'The grass is gone, too. Look, not a blade, leaf or petal.' The track is a dozen feet wide and not much grows on it, anyway, so the absence of greenery in that circle wasn't hugely obvious at first sight.

'I don't believe it,' Archie was staring down. 'Folk don't just disappear on a footpath. Not one as wide as this, practically straight, with solid woods both sides, and no side-paths off.'

'*They* did,' I insisted.

'I never even saw'em.'

We walked round the perimeter of the bald patch. 'You must have; just back there, when you were taking pics of the squirrel and those great tits at the feeder. You can't have been concentrating so much you never even saw them walk right past us? You didn't even notice the longest-legged girl in the nation?'

'Ah… yes… And the shortest shorts, too. I do vaguely remember,' he confessed. 'They must have just walked faster than we realised. They'll be down past the curve.'

He was only saying it to convince himself. I looked down the trail where the rail line from the coal mine had run a hundred years ago – now a shaded walk. We could see four hundred yards before the slight curve would hide anyone.

'You'd think there'd be ants and insects in there…' I peered.

Someone was just coming into sight. A couple with a dog, along the trackway where the trees arched completely across, like a green-lit tunnel. 'No. Nobody could have walked that far that quick. There aren't even any leaves or twigs there,' I said. 'Perfectly clean circle.'

'You'll be telling me the worms have gone, too.'

The dog-walking duo paused as they came close, 'Wassup then?'

'Three youngsters came walking past us. Disappeared somewhere round here.'

'They came past you, did they?' Archie's persistent when he latches on to an idea.

They shook their heads, 'You're the first we've seen.'

'Must have cut through the trees,' Archie was looking round hopefully.

'There's no side paths till the end, at the old tower.'

We all shrugged and ummed and ahhed and I gave the dog the dead-eye when it thought about being my friend.

'Okay, alright, see ya.' We stepped away so they could come past, keeping well to the right, still socially-distancing.

'Yeah, cheers, see y—'

'Eh?' They'd gone. Not so much as a puff of smoke. I was gob-smacked – in the current God-awful vernacular. 'We... I... They...' I pointed.

Archie turned, 'Where they gone?'

'Dunno. Up there?' I pointed through the overhanging branches.

We both automatically sniffed – still the burning smell. 'Might be a bit stronger now?' I wondered.

Archie gave in, 'Now *they've* definitely vanished. Into thin air. Yeah. Okay.'

So I called 999 while Archie marked the edge of the ten-foot circle with a stick, carving a rough groove out, while keeping well out of the ring.

Naturally, the police go-between on the phone told me I was wasting their time and could be prosecuted if I persisted. And the line went dead. So Archie rang, and he knows how to give people a rollicking. So they put the phone down on him, too. So we rang again, and I said there'd been an explosion and people were injured, 'And the police should come as well as an ambulance.'

It took an hour, and by then we had a little congregation of a dozen or so walkers clustered round the dusty circle. Most of them were pretty dubious, but willing to wait to see what the fuzz would do – with us, if not the circle.

The two police and two paramedics were not happy bunnies at having to walk half a mile along the track to reach us. 'It's nicely shaded,' I consoled them. 'For such a hot day.'

But they were beyond listening to mere members of the public. 'No evidence of a fire or explosion.' They conferred. 'Wasting police time.' I heard several times.

'I never mentioned a fire,' I protested. 'But just look inside the circle: it's all dead and dry.'

'Book'em,' someone called.

'Even the grass is gone,' Archie joined in.

'There's no grass anywhere along the track. It's practically sterile.'

'So you raked it all away. This is a serious offence, Sir and Madam,' Senior Policeman told us, very sternly.

'Names,' said the other one, stepping closer.

'Don't go in the circle,' I said, panicking.

He sneer-laughed, 'Don't try that on—' Junior Policeman was gone.

Talk about stupefied. 'What you done with...?' the senior one tailed off, gaining an inkling of how stupid he sounded.

Surprise and satisfaction littered the faces of the onlookers. 'Wouldn't be told,' they knowingly agreed. 'Won't be the last, you see.'

Sure enough, the big strapping paramedic was heading across scratched-out perimeter, fixed on me and Archie. He turned to glass – see-through – for around two nanoseconds, not having time to be surprised, and he'd gone.

Junior sidekick policeman foolishly followed, and vanished the same. 'Dimbo,' someone said, edging back a couple more feet.

The young lady paramedic had more sense than her three former colleagues put together. Looking very shaken, she got on the phone, though why she turned away to not let us hear, I'll never know, but she did, and we all heard, anyway, through her semi-hysterics.

So we waited again. Somebody went back up the track to fetch some rope from the stables, and we started to tie it across the trackway, when this jogger came belting down – as they do – thump-thumping feet, headphones on, oblivious to the rest of the universe, vaulting over the rope and vanishing up his own oblivion. He was swiftly followed by a manic biker who shouldn't have been along there, anyway, so nobody was especially bothered.

So we had it all cordoned off, and we were hanging round waiting for the backup police. You'd have thought eight vanishings would be enough to convince anyone. But no. There's no accounting for the mischievousness, or outright arrogance, of kids who duck under the rope, sneering at the lot of us. Not to mention their overweight and fully hysterical mother who went straight through the rope and disappeared. 'No loss,' said Mr Renshaw who owns the Chippy. 'They live next door to me… Er, *lived.*'

Police reinforcements arrived. Flooding up the trackway, out of breath, Chiefy talking to Lady Paramed who was calm now – getting over her fluster with some Haribos I gave her. She gabbled away and pointed at me and Archie, and to the ropes and the circle. 'No! Don't—'

Too late. Senior Officer knew best. It was written all over him that ropes, cordons and the general public didn't apply to him. He trod the rope down, tripped, staggered a couple of steps into Archie's circle.

'Ring of Death, twelve,' Mr Renshaw said. 'People, nil.'

189

That seemed to do it. 'Everybody back!' Another one was ordering as all back, and told me and Archie to remain and all the others to go away. 'There's nothing to see.' He was right there – three police officers, for a start, were not to be seen any longer. So of course, this daft old couple who live at the back of us come straight over the rope that Chiefy trod down. 'We live that way,' he's saying. 'We'd never manage to walk all the way round.'

'I wonder which of them was Unlucky Thirteen?'

'Whichever, fourteen wasn't any less unlucky.'

'Nothing to do with luck. Senility.'

So we gave full statements. More of them were turning up. Armed ones. 'Expecting terrorists?' I asked, innocently.

'Or aliens?'

'Time travellers?' We were all full of helpful suggestions.

'If your soldiers are going to throw themselves into the woods and lie down and crawl a lot, they should be careful – the dog walkers turn their little jewels loose in there for do-do duty.'

But they charged into the wood on both sides, got tangled in barbed wire, broke the old fence down, scared all the rabbits squirrels and birds, shouted a lot, and rather unceremoniously sent us away.

'Eff off, you two.'

We've had four visits from the police and some army people since then. I have learned how pointless it is to tell them anything, because the next one wants us to say it all again. 'Like replays of Rambo, you are.' I told the last pair, and I won't be offering them cream cakes again.

Two lots of parents have been to visit us, too – mystified and distraught. The long-legged girl and the other two youngsters.

The policeman's wife came. She was almost thanking us for not warning him. 'We *did* warn him,' I was indignant about that. 'But he still trod the rope down and walked over it.'

'Been doing that to me for years,' she said. 'No harm done, eh?' Pleasant little smile she had.

The track, of course, is still closed. We thus have no quick way down to the river. The army is camped in the park, about a hundred of them. So no kids' recreation in the village, other than tormenting soldiers in various ways, from the boys throwing horse dung, to the girls lifting skirts with the same sexy little flick that I used to use myself. Mr Renshaw's Chippy has opened an extension, and has a huge marquee for sit-downers. The army doesn't mix with the sciencey or police lots, or the increasing near-horde of tourists – fourteen yesterday.

There's an eighteen-foot-high mesh and electric fence round Archie's little circle – except it's now four hundred yards diameter. They cut a lot of trees down, until they realised that everybody could then see what they were doing.

Rumour has it that two more scientist types have gone to infinity and beyond. And we think they tried to send something else – like a bomb, perhaps – but it didn't disappear. 'Probably because it wasn't alive. We could have told them that in the first two minutes,' I said.

'They have to learn for themselves.' Archie said, trying to open a parcel from Amazon.

There was a lot of fuss when they tried to send that scieency-bomb thing, whatever it was. Lots of flashing and lights and huge bangs that shook the Chippy. Some folk thought there was a funny burning smell, too. 'And it's not the Chippy this time.'

They've started on a three-storey building on Jenkins' back meadow. Bit silly because it floods every winter. And it looks as if they're constructing one of those geodesic domes that looks like a football. We think it's over Archie's circle.

Never a single official word on the telly, of course. "Declined to comment" is the best we get, although the rumour-mill around the village is rife with ideas about it being a black hole – that's actually our neighbours across the road – or a time gate, or a portal to a parallel world. The pub down the end, The Brinsley Manor, has renamed itself the Brinsley Time-Gate, and is enjoying a customer-boom now. Except for the army, who they won't let in after that to-do last weekend.

'Parallel World? I should have tried it while I had the chance,' Archie says. But that's just when I'm getting on to him about doing the garden.

Anyway, that's the background to explain to you members of the parish council why you need to approve the diversion of the footpath around the big wire fence, preferably before the summer's finished.

I'm Enid Pearson, and thank you again for your time.

THE TANGERINE AFFAIR

'It's a Tangerine for Pit's sake. Myry Maxadorr is a Tanga, an alien.' Lord! How often do I have to re-state the totally self-evident? 'I'm hardly going to be having an affair with a jelly-based metre-high, metre-wide orange bag with eighteen eyes in a double row, and a set of feathery-antennae on top, now am I? Sure, I like her. Got a lot in common, we have. *Interests*, not anything else.'

I looked around them, all staring at me with dubious, disbelieving expressions on their faces – and their para-seque, too, in the case of the Koyns among them.

'And yet... and yet... that's what you're accusing me of – having carnal relations with a Tangerine? How? What kinda perverted minds inhabit your bodies, you Gov guys?'

It's not that I'm against close relations with any of the other species out there... or down here on Miscela, as often as not. Except I wouldn't know what to fancy about a Tanga. Myry's quite juicy, I know – I squeezed her once when she tried to get through a narrow doorway. Tasty, as well, from what little experience I've had...

Or, what would anyone do with a quarter-mecho? They have no obvious orifices. Yoidles – it'd be like sticking it in a meat-grinder and seeing if anyone pressed the start button. That's if you could find the right place, anyway. As for the double-tailers or the chits – let's not go there. Beautiful minds, but weird thought-patterns, or *emotraces*, as one tried to explain to me – I spent a semester trying to understand them. Don't know if it got me far. Difficult to say if you're not fluent in emotranics – and my command of it is more mystery than mastery.

This accusation of my supposed Affair with a Tanga even went to *The Shimmers* – the ultimate arbiters of law and governance in the KayYu. No – the *Kay Yu* – the Known Universe. Obviously. Effinell.

As we all know, they ain't got bodies to house their curling, gleaming minds. Sitting there – as much as you know what bodiless beings do – maybe not sitting *per se*, they just sort of hung there at this hearing I had to attend. Or simply *were* there, hovering – shimmering in the air. Ghostlike gods, the Ultimates.

I've never seen one before. There might have been several, or lots. Who can tell? You just know something's there. It's really like I'd always heard – there's something formless moving sinuously in front of you, indefinable. I think I detected three patches of gleaming, shifting air in the room. Weird. Really quite something – an experience, anyway.

They adjudicated, so-called – it's all their own publicity, I reckon. They hovered and almost invisibly wraithed in the air; and it felt like they logged into my head. I had so much respect for them – it's bred into us – they are the Gods-among-us. And I never actually had anything to do with them in person before; practically mythical to the average likes of me. *And anyway,* I was arguing with myself, *what would be wrong with it if I was in any kind of physical relationship with a Tanga? Or any other non-humanic species? I mean, like stalkies or chits or Koyns?*

I thought cross-species relations were encouraged? Even admitting I had an open mind seemed like I was pleading guilty to something terrible. I felt the tickle in my mind, like tiny ice-cubes tingling inside me – that was peculiar. 'That means they heard you,' somebody said. But I hardly got the feeling they gave me a hearing.

The verdict was pronounced – Guilty – in capital letters, neon-lit glitter, underlined and advertised on the KUWeb. *Guilty! Me!* Like I could be guilty of anything except of having faith in justice, fairness, truth. Yoidles! Was that misplaced, or what? All wiped away now. Shimmers? Godlike beings that understand all? Huh. To think how much I revered them in the past, believed all the hype about higher existences that understand all. What a load of anti-me shiko. Once you're up there, you create your own publicity, and then start to believe it.

Back of my mind, I'm still thinking – Even if there had been anything physical between me and Myry Maxadorr, so the chuff what? Nothing of that nature is illegal. Maybe that's what the shimmers tagged onto, in my head –

seditionist thinking. And let it bias their judgement. Shimmering shikos.

My wife believes it, for Suhgar's sake. *My wife!* Five foot seven, with boobs and mind I adore. Blonde and gorgeous. I could not possibly dream of having an affair with anyone or anything else. She is everything to me – apart from my kids – who I worship. Not saints, but perfect kids – not really kids any longer – late teens and having their own socio-sexual problems

Myry Maxadorr, on the other hand... has a charming, wonderful mind. She is amazing – what she thinks. *How* she thinks. I mean, her thoughts are works of beauty. But she's a giant tangerine, or perhaps a satsuma – three of her eyes are a touch slitty. How the Dorks in Dovvon am I supposed to have some illicit torrid affair with a Tanga? To be honest, I wouldn't have the slightest idea how, or where, to start. And what would be illicit about it? Yes, yes, I know, I go on about it. But it gets to me.

'I demand the right to appeal,' I told them. Several times. Loudly. Vainly. I gained the idea that the shimmers did the appeals process, such as it was, and they upheld their own decision without a thought.

It was the politicos from the Bureau of Interspecies Integration who came demanding my document case – the one I always have with me. My private case. All my stuff in it. My private stuff – diaries; appointments; plazz, cat pads, keys, chippers – innermost stuff. I refused. Not their business. My intimate stuff. I'm honest in there. My open-heart stuff. It's not just my research and work stuff, which, at the time, was delving into tangerines – no, not the fruit – the orange-ball aliens from Tanga.

196

That research was what they wanted, the interfering demons. It was official GovDep research, for chuffsake. All approved, with my reports going in weekly – vids, evidence mountings, conclusions to date and everything. But somebody was reading something more into it.

It's not as if the Tangas are sexual: they are semi-clones. They divide themselves, and lay whichever piece is smallest into a hollow – or nowadays, into a specially-excavated pond or bath. Then any other ripe one in the area can deposit their smaller portions in there as well, and they merge... or not. Could be more than two – it's a slow process, and fairly random. And not complete until growth triggers a barrier-skin formation. Until then, there could be multiple contributors making several individuals – each retaining different characteristics and memories – very much a unified mind. A portion of shared thinking, anyway. Seems to work for them. Anyway, that was what I was researching. All official. It was GovDep sponsored, for chuffsake.

Then one day GovDep sent me this Update Brief – same as every Thongday – all the usual alerts and reminders; emphasise this, not that. Bit more... "In pursuance of genetic breeding research goals, you are requested to add your DNA in with theirs at the next opportunity."

'Eh?' I said. 'What does that mean? How?'

'Ejaculate your seed in the bath with theirs,' came the answer.

'You want me to stand next to a bath with a couple of Tanga segments in it, while they're merging, and have a wank? Never.'

'It's experimental. You need to get your timing right – to add your genetic matter in the middle period of their

197

fusion, when they're absorbing each other's material. Purely an experiment.'

'Not with me, it's not. I observe, not participate. I'd be fathering – or mothering – cross-breed carrot-coloured aliens for your test vats. In-vitro aliens.' I was becoming really worked-up at the whole idea. 'It ain't gonna happen. No, never. You're not getting the chance to do experiments with my kids – even if they look like shelly tadpoles. Attractive to some, maybe – not me. You'd stir-fry them and dump them in the pond. Or in the blender and down the drain, whatever.

'No; it's not happening.' I downed tools, with some finality. 'I might develop fatherly feelings towards them – I'd have some emotional attachment to them, as well as bio-genetic.'

Basically, I think that was what started all this off about me and Myry. I reckon it was them at the GovDep office who stirred it all up with the Non-Indigene Bureau when some of them went round to the Tanga HQ, supposedly enquiring about me not being cooperative. I was pretty sure they simply turned the shoat loose on me, because sure enough, GovDep believed all sorts of things about me not cooperating with the NIB; not wanting to follow the research path; not dedicated. That got the Tangas all worked up and spiteful. They got their antennae in a twist, all round their necks, except they didn't have necks. Suddenly convinced I wouldn't cooperate, they accused me of being guilty of "Unauthorised Breeding Effort."

'No effort to me,' I said. 'I didn't do anything. I refused. Come on, I work closely with Myry. She has a wonderful mind; I would really like to get closer to her intellectual patterns. I think you Tangas are something to really learn from. I'd love to—'

'Thank you for your contribution to date, Vytor. We have your official acknowledgement for your thumb-print; You will guarantee to—' I didn't hear any more of their demands – I'd have to do something, and never do something else. Never speak about my affair... cease my other TangaGov Research and business... Whatever.

I could only guess they drugged me that time I was in their labs for the updating day. And extracted semen.

I expect somebody could prove something about my D_2NA being in the Tanga's new-borns. But there's no way I could afford to have their carroty little tadpoles D_2NA-tested. I say "little" – they're at least the size of a beachball, and they're probably off-planet by now. And, whatever the tests showed, they'd use it to prove whatever they wanted.

Thus I'm out in the cold. I keep getting the irrational feeling that everyone's conspiring against me – all with different motives and angles. Or no motive and the same angle, I'm not clear on that. So now, my wife got the shimmers to issue an exclusion order against me, so I can't get in at home, even to see the kids, or talk to her. No appeal, it's a total mess – a totalitarian mess. I'm in with the dregs... the gutter. I sleep rough. Can't get in the shelters – I'm outcast. All I get is vindictive shrugs, like I did everything in the universe wrong from the Wreck of the Edmondo Fizz Herald to the Konnort Rebellion. I can't even figure why both the Tangans and the humanics are chorked with me. I did nothing. *They* did it.

They thanked me, officially. Then cast me out to the yoggs, complete with certificate of thanks and a Notice of Impending Action under the "Deviant Behaviours Act of 21347" – last week. I understand that it refers to practices likely to bring the universe into disrepute.

I'm really confused. Their gratitude and vilification in equal measure, all for something *they* did, not me. Somebody got their wires crossed, and it's not just a couple of quarter-mechs. *They* would do it right – you want a job doing right, ask a Qmech – they think in details. They're great company for drinking with, too: they always buy the first round, like an honour thing with them, 'Wonderful trait to have in a friend,' I always tell them.

I'm not going downhill – I'm already there.

I met these guys in the boxes under the launch platform where the sharp gravity anomalies caused by take-offs warm the plascrete up a bit. Yeah – so a few downer-guys get freaked-up inside their heads. They don't know, so it doesn't matter to them. Small price to pay for being warm, and finding scraps to eat among the waste and toss-outs. We get all sorts down there – quite a few very affable stalkies who tell incomprehensible jokes to each other all the time. I worked with'em a year or two back, so I heard all the jokes before but they liked it that I laughed at the right places.

And a quarter-mech bunch. We even had a couple of chitins for a few nights – absolutely interesting, they were. I never spent a lot of informal time with them before – plenty of day-time work, but not what you might think of as leisure – in the crawl-space under the launch pads. Eye-opening stuff with them guys.

Right menagerie, it is. We all doss down together – it's warmer that way. And no bother – not even with a pair of double-tailers in season. We don't share food, though. Experidrugs, yes, but not food.

'Try this, it'll free up your spirit,' these Koyns told me, passing round a whiffer. 'Couple of the other guys recommended it.' Bit of a sly look so I knew there was something, but what the Sugh? You have a few bevvs and a smoke, and your troubles are in the ether and you got nowhere special to be. So I was up for it; I'd known a few Koyns before all this. But the Koyns were granted independence, and the Imperial forces departed. So this place, the old Empire Space Camp, has been mostly deserted since. They'll be looking for new firms to move in when they're sure it's safe, what with all the munitions that were left.

Odd things, the Koyns, semi-chitinous with their multi-joints, but I always found them okay. Sense of humour, some high thinkers among them. Aspects of their techno-mechanicals are brill. I did a research project on their thinking styles a few years back. Yeah, I really liked'em.

Boy! That whiffer I sucked on! I dream-drifted to the waft of the next spirit-freeing drag I took. 'Free it, man,' I told myself, and almost laughed.

It never seriously occurred to me I could come to any harm; I mean, we were all taking something, and passing round and passing out and trying something different every time we resurfaced. 'Anything to pass these bitter-cold nights, eh?'

Chits, clickies, softies like me, Koyns… anyone and anything, really. You have to get on with everybody under the launch plates, whoever it was, they all needed temporary comfort among us

Some stalky had filched a load of gear from a place he raided. So he said, anyway, and it was him and his colly who were saying how this stuff was *goooood*, 'Not much of it about; freeee y' spirit, man.' They always say "man" when they're pre-spaced themselves. So I wasn't troubled in the least when I was drifting all euphoric and seeing stars and turkuuls... tangerines and women... and dishes of carrotede with jugs of ale and bixies.

Lights going bright and soft, slow-changing, different colours, I was dreaming through this session, thinking, 'That's Tanga taste for theme atmospherics – nice, like floating and settling among all these Koyns crouching round like they do. 'Free your spirit, man...' echoing through me... 'Freeee your soul.'

I was awake. Laid out... Like in the middle of the party. Faces all round me, bodies, too, and I'm lying down. Can't move – alien faces all round, three Tangas as well as all the Koyns. Couple of stalkies. I can't read them – they're all inscrutable.

I'm getting a bit desperate to be in the thinking-pool with them. *I need to tune in.* Can feel them poking at me. I'm naked, surrounded by other items – can't see. They're eating the other bits – it's food dishes all round me.

So am I – they're laughing and tucking in... start ripping bits off me... eating me!!! Alive; tearing and slicing slices off me; laughing and chattering as though it were nothing. I'm just a different dish. No!!!! Not that. Food for them!!! I'm a delicacy!

When I'm dreaming, I never think, "This is a dream". And I didn't then. This's no dream, and it's not a soul-freeing drug launch, either. This's real – I feel the cuts, the rips. I'm raw, for Suhgar's sake! You can't eat me raw. I'd know if I was cooked. I'm screaming and shrieking and struggling and not moving a muscle or an eyelash and I feel my blood draining; my brain's fading; shuy shay shoy!!! They're killing me, eating me alive!!! 'You gotta stop…stop… stop…'

I'm dying. Must be dead. Except I'm not. I can raise my head – but they took my eyes and one of the Tangas was still squelching on them. I still see – it *is* a dream. But it isn't – I see down my body: it's ravaged, torn open, apart. My ribs are cracked apart, lifted and parted. One's got his mandibles gnawing along a rack of my ribs. A greenish Koyn with a twisted palp has my heart, mincing it in its jaws, dipping strips of thigh flesh in some purple-coloured gunge.

I'm seeing it all from higher now. Loosening, as though I'm sitting up. 'You gotta stop. Put it back.' One's spitting bits out, joking about something – toe and finger bones. I'm a bloodied mess – bones and gristle. Seeing from higher, like from standing: my head is open – the top lifted free – my brain in the open cup of skull – mushed. One of the Tangas is scooping cup-paws of it into its jaws.

'Free your spirit,' they'd said. It didn't mean the smokes… or the hoosh… the whiffer… but something else. They'd known about this, had they? At least some of it. I could turn away, look around. I was drifting, sailing up, as though suddenly set loose, ties with my carcass cut. 'Am I really dead? Is my soul going to get dragged to heaven or hell any mo now? Will I be launched into a tangerine orbit? Or come back as a chɪt?' Asking myself, and receiving no answers.

Drifting… 'Does anyone in the banquet room know what's truly happening to me? Or do the under-crete guys at the anti-grav pad?' I raised a hand – nothing there. Felt at my face – nothing. Patted my body down – just air. I'm panicking, whirling. 'I'm having no effect on anyone, or anything there. You'd think they didn't know…'

But they'd said, 'Free your spirit.' Somebody must know this's happening. Going frantic, I'm dashing round, trying to get back into my carcass. But it's ripped apart, dismembered and bloodily emptied – barely half of me left. I'm too vile to go near, even for me. Can't approach them, either – I pass through them. I try to click into place in their bodies, but nothing happens. *So it's not a take-over mechanism.*

Ghastly, and lost in complete internal panic, I'm sinking; absolute despair – cast into the darkness, drifting away from the me-fest down there. Lost in the fading laughter among the Koyns and Tangas.

So strange. Dark and quiet. I'm drifting. Seeing dark shapes – the other people around me – Tangas, Koyns… a few stalkies. A scattering of others – chits. I tried to wave to them, speak to them. They never saw me… or felt anything when I attempted to touch them. A lot of humans, too. But I didn't know where I was, drifting through the rooms, and out, around buildings, along the streets. Wondering if I could find home, I tried to go another way, not be carried by each waft of air.

I managed to resist the drift-along current a little… almost bumped into a Koyn.

'Oh, awesome. Yoiks, was that a Shimmer?' I heard it say that, but I was drifting onward.

'What? Where?'

'Didn't you see it?'

'You're imagining things, Degs. I never saw anything.' Their voices faded away.

What were they saying? About me?

Another voice, close by. 'Here you are.' I turn slowly. Nothing's there. It wasn't a voice, merely a thought within my head.

'We expected you to become free later, Vytor; to drift for longer.' A voice, disembodied.

Am I like that? 'What are you?' I asked the emptiness around me.

'You must know.'

Other voices, eerie, almost echoing. 'You will become one of us.'

'You will need to wander and seek—'

'Seek what? Who are you? Where are you?'

'You will come to understand so much. You need to learn so much.'

'You were chosen.'

'Chosen? This was all planned? What for?'

'Chosen because you already have so much understanding of the races and species; so much empathy.'

'Superbly qualified to begin this journey.' The voices around me piled one on top of the other.

I'm being shimmered, I thought. 'Don't I get any choice? What happened to my free will? I'm entitled—'

'No, I'm afraid you're not. No-one could *choose* to be one of us. We are born so to be. As were you.'

'No, no. I'm a lingual researcher. I compare ways of thinking—'

'You enjoy it, and you're extremely good at it.'

'You're likeable, you relate with all kinds of beings. It's the perfect grounding.'

'Almost as though you chose yourself.'

'Come, link with me while we begin.'

I reached outward, as though I had some substance again, and made slight contact – a shock – I was held, magnet-like, to another. To one of the voices – a formless being.

The bond was strong, holding us together as I was led towards the light.

'Always in the company of one or other of us in the beginning,' the voice returned, 'you will learn. To become a shimmer.'

TOKEN

'Upea, you are magnificent.' The times I've said that to her. I was in absolute awe of her – so tall and so slender, long-necked, she seemed to sway above me like a gold-eyed hoverbird. That iridescent green-gold skin; and her smile was to die for – her eyes almost lit up in the most beautiful amber. Course, I'm only the token human companion; having me as a close companion shows cross-species solidarity.

'I chose you myself from the vidz of Availables that were sent me,' she told me not long after I'd started with her. 'I'm certainly not the sort to have permitted anyone else to do the selection for me.'

And, as time went by, we became closer than simply leader and candy. As she once said, 'There are times, Yaff, when we seem to have a near-telepathic understanding.'

We'd chatter and relax; eat together, even drink. I'd escort her to all her art performance events near home, and when travelling. I'd wait in the foyers and vestibules of such places – that was my main public role – as the equality-oriented decoration. I never once questioned my role: I'd known in advance exactly what was expected of me.

I'd be there to greet guests, or guide her towards the presences she desired to meet socially, or for her business – if you can call artistry a business.

'She is the most talented irrid I've ever met,' I tell anyone who'll listen. 'Or seen on the vivvies. Her works are reproductions of herself – each one a musical and visual masterpiece.' Her music-art performances told mystic stories that people – irrids, humans and clozies alike – adored. As much as anything, that was because everyone experienced them as a personally-directed happening that varied subtly with every replay.

When her performance was under way, I might be invited to the kitchens or servants' hall, where everyone craved for the inside word about her. All I could tell was the absolute truth, 'I love everything about her – her beauty on the surface and within, her talent, her humour, her… her everything. She's not the only irrid I've known closely, but she's an orbit above all the others.'

'And she's getting better and better – everyone says so,' they all used to tell me. 'We thought she was wonderful before, but this past year, she's taken on a whole new level; as though she's inspired. Not you, is it?' They'd nudge and nod, wanting some intimacy from me.

'Not me, I'm a companion. Merely a token nod to the species mix.'

'Some token.'

'You make a good pair,' they'd say, but, while there was truth in that, it was only the surface. Our relationship never delved any deeper; there were no hidden depths with us. I supported her, did all I could, and quietly worshipped her.

Contentment was the least of my feelings, to be with Upea in that position. And she was happy that I was there, 'I'm getting better,' she told me. 'I'm seeing new ways, new dreams. See how they flock and clamour to see me.'

One day, 'Yaff,' she said, 'Take my hand.' And we walked from the transo along the blue and gold paradeway into the theatre gallery for a premier of her latest poetic musical perfection. It had a name I found unpronounceable until I spent an evening training it into my mind and thinking of it in terms of a musical phrase. Ever since, I almost sing it when I say it; I've even been complimented on my rendition of it – 'Amazingly good." I could tell they missed out the "for a human" bit, but that was okoi.

It was not long after my year's contract had terminated, and Upea had asked me to stay on. 'I leapt at it,' I told Miriki in the Lounge Club. I was welcomed into the rather exclusive society these days, having accompanied Upea there on many occasions. 'I'd do anything to stay with her. I've saved enough to do it for nothing, simply to share with her. She has such beauty of spirit and form that I bathe in, glory in. I know she lifts me to new heights.' I've even seen her naked several times and she is— Well, I could never say, not to anyone.

I was almost on the edge of the vivvy-light after that walk together down the blue and gold. We were postered all over the Nets – close-ups and everything. They wanted me to do interviews, but I couldn't – I might slip and say something wrong, something she wouldn't like, or they'd simply make up my answers and offerings and re-animate their library pics of me.

The occurrence wasn't of whole-public interest across the planet, of course, but it entranced and captivated those who were into such matters. Only among our circle – *her* circle, I mean, all fifty-two million of her active followers. I suppose we did look okoi together – though our hand-holding was perhaps a step too far down the parade for some – irrids and humans just don't.

She took my hand again several times, at lesser occasions. I didn't raise the subject in our leisure evenings alone, and nor did she. So something was left unspoken, and only understood by one of us. Even our near telepathy had only a feel of warmth and... and *affection* to it; nothing more.

I continued to wait in reception areas and anterooms, but that was fine – I was almost a celebrity among my fellow servants and companions, whether human, clozie or irrid.

Often, as we chattered and nibbled, relaxed and played, I had fleeting wonderings about her motivations, although I never once allowed my thoughts to tingle ahead in any particular direction. I deliberately closed my ears and mind to them when such matters were jested about in the waiting times.

Still she smiled and even laughed; still I adored and accompanied – revelling in my life and not looking to develop it or change it. Of course, I wondered about some of the human girls I met – young women in similar positions to mine, or independent earners and agents. I knew I could match up with some of them, but it wouldn't have a future – not with Upea and I travelling so much. One nighters, they'd be, maybe occasional five or ten-nighters away. Sometimes, I stayed in her room with her, and sometimes in an adjoining room, or even a separate suite – depending on something I wasn't privy to. And a couple of occasions, I was moved out for undisclosed reasons.

One day, 'I have a special set of clothes for you to wear at tonight's event – a black suit with iridescent amber pelisse. It's the same depth of amber as my eyes,' she said.

'Bit over-smart for the walk down the paradeway,' two of the hangers-on ribbed. 'Maybe she's going to take you inside – to the event.'

'I mean – a one-shoulder golden jacket...' they winked and smiled. 'You'll look quite something in that.'

Yeah, right. Inside? As if. I'd only once glimpsed the inside of one of the halls when an event was on – they were almost exclusively irrid affairs, with an occasional human or clozie companion or independent. Was she intending to take me into this one with her? I'd never thought that high – not seriously, anyway.

We'd had a meal together the previous evening, and I'd stayed in her room. We'd shared a few after-drinks and played Fun Strata. So sparkly-eyed, she'd been, as though on guintahol. That broad smile from the heavens.

Maybe… maybe… might she?

'Ai, yes, you look perfect, Yaff,' she greeted me.

She was right – the pelisse and her eyes were an exact match. 'Come,' and held her hand for me to take. It seemed we almost floated along the carpetta and stairs into the atrium, where we were greeted by the Matria and retinue and where I would always feel the slight flick of her wrist, a symbolic casting off – the signal for me to step aside.

It came. I was expecting it. Of course. I let go instantly. I stepped to the side and gave a slight bow to the Welcome Group, and waited for her to go in. More than a mite disappointed – I'd almost believed she would. I'd let myself hope. For the first time. To go Inside.

She turned from the group – such glorious iridescence from her skin, those eyes so huge and amber, perfectly matching my pelisse. Had I thought beyond? Some message in the amber match of her eyes? She turned them to me. Did my heat surge in hope? Dammit, yes. I soared at the thought, the dream. She came closer. That smile looking down and meeting my mud-green eyes, 'You fawning, cowering, timid little creature. What despair I sense in your breast. Did you dare hope? And plan?' Such

211

derision flooded from her smiling lips and eyes, 'The best-laid schemes of clozie and men so often drain away, and you're left with nought but grief and pain for the joy you schemed and promised yourself.'

The gorgeous smile was a sneering smirk. From Upea! I smiled and nodded in automaton mode. My world was crashing. Disintegrating, as she bade farewell, 'I don't need you any longer, little man,' and spun away towards the inner hall, 'however much Impressar Pravda tells me I do.'

My being crumbled within, dribbled to the maho in trickles of dust. I thought it was truly happening and my perspective would sink and fade and they'd sweep me away.

But still I stood. A blank mind on a paper body on trembling legs that moved and turned and went away and found themselves in the underhall and sat and wept emptily within and remained stone-faced and unmoving for an age of darkness and blurred shapes that spoke and moved and offered and asked. But I had no answer or response.

The call to return to the reception never came – the other escorts went and I was alone. With the home servants and a few overnighters whom I never saw.

There I remained.

Bereft of soul, I awoke. There was an attempt to eat a fast-break. I didn't take part.

The Magniffa at the pseudodesk had my belongings in a remarkably small and neat cluster, with a complimentary bag.

'No – she left early this morning.'

'Home, I imagine...'

'No, no ticket for you. There was this...'

His turquoise fingerlings handed me a card. My blank gaze told me nothing, but I knew. It would be my wages… with bonus, perhaps. And/or severance payoff. It would be generous. Or not. As if it would matter. After almost two years with nothing and no-one else, now, I had no *Her*.

I shrank and went, and stayed shrunken – no longer the human lauded in mind and body. My gloss-black hair went lank and dry. I pulled it out and shaved it off – the old way of penance back home. Unbothered by eating, my muscles wasted. Bent over, I didn't see the panels that fell from high when the wind grew, and one shattered in front of me and slashed my face and I lost an eye.

I bought another, a pale blue one, like an ice cave. 'Just to be different,' I told Lele-Anna, a girl who spoke with me in a Sarafon dinerbar that was cheap, had humanic food, and customers like her.

'But actually,' I confessed, 'it was all they had in stock. I see again, but there's little to look at, especially in the mirror.'

I cluttered by; stayed in Sarafon for a while, half a year and half a world away from Her, doing little but wander and shamble by.

My main possessions arrived in a small container one day. I sent them away. They were *Her*.

'Let's move to Treng.' Lele-Anna asked me. We'd drunk and eaten a few times in a couple of dinerbars. More than a few. 'Come on,' she cajoled. 'There's nothing here for you. I'm going to set up my soul-reading salon, and they're reckoned to be receptive sort of people in Treng. We get on, don't we? I like having you round. You kind of, I dunno, raise my efforts. What say, hmm?'

So I went with her, and recalled the times Upea and I had stayed in Treng, at the HiRaffa, or at the Regenta.

But Lele-Anna and I didn't lodge close to either, though I saw *Her* on the vivvies a few times – on news items, or a concerta evening of her latest works. Strange, I wasn't as impressed as I used to be, thinking *She's lost her glow; her shine is a touch dulled and the tones stilted where they should be spiralling* – as my soul had soared so often with the brilliance of her musical moods and poetic shapes and tales.

I heard not a word of the same. All was praise and extolation on the plax and the vivvies. *Maybe it's just me, not seeing her with the same infatuated, rosine eyes.*

Lele-Anna thought it was me feeling jaded, 'It sounded okoi to me, but I'm not into it anyway – got a couple of hers on my experipad, that's all.'

She worked as an independent diviner and healer, and we set up a lodge-front salon on Side-Main Street in Treng, and she did her readings and divinings, held séance-style sessions with the living of all three species, and had a steady clientele pass-through. She was so graceful and deep-seeing, and I just sort of helped around – took the weight off her feet, or her shoulders, not sure which. Things were going okoi and we got on fine and her salon was doing good and picking up and I used to hand little lectro-cards out and buy the drinks on slow days.

'Yaff! Yaff!' She was in late one day, 'I got a stand at the Regia Stadium! Some massive concert on; it's to be an all-day special festival fair, where they have lots of stand-holders to help make it a worthwhile, wide-interest, whole-day experience for the visitors.'

**

214

Lele-Anna had a porto-lectro-stand and we set it up together, watching the throng of well-manicured attendees parade past us, stare and mutter, enquire or walk on. Or come in to check us out – to check Lele-Anna out. Visitors of all persuasions – irrids, clozies, humans and another one we didn't know, but it had a retinue with it.

I stayed with her for all the day, just to hang about, make the scuff'n'coff, the bickies, keep re-mounting the holo-poster that was continually dropping from the wall, and give out a few hundred fliers I'd run up.

But, as much as anything, I stayed all through the day and evening for fear of a lone day and night. The prospect so unappealed. 'If I have one more cold grey night alone, I'll only drown myself in drink and self-distaste.' So Lele-Anna's invitation was timely; it probably saved my drunken collapse off the top of our tower that night

While she sessioned with the self-doubting clients, and eased their minds and showed them their inner hopes, I wandered around the hall and huge foyer, among all the other day-stands, giving away our hand-out cards, feeling no more than morose disinterest; seeing little of all the wares and gadgets on display and sale – the artistry, the delicacies, the clothing, the music... the imported glassware and ancient artefacts.

'I was surprised to be granted a space in the first place,' Le-an confessed. 'But Mr Ada, one of the organisers, said a friend happened to visit the salon, and had mentioned me as a rising star, following a truly uplifting session with me. I don't know who it was, or even if it was an irrid or whatever. He'd been vastly impressed with his reading, apparently. And he loved my gift of a smoke-glass with music tones that we formed together – a reflection of his inner self.

'I did a session with Mr Ada, as a sort of vetting thing. He loved my reading, and the sculpture gift that we created, and asked if I would like to join the circuit as one of the regular invitees.

'He took my open mouth as a yes; and I'm in! Yaff! I'm in!'

Delighted for her – hugging, squeezing together. Jeeps, my joy for her was uplifting – so thrilled for her.

'You'll do so well, Le-an; so well. I'll tell folk I knew you as a beginner; toured with you in the early days. Jod! I'm so pleased for you.' I hadn't realised I could possibly feel like that. I'd had no thought resembling it in the near-year since Upea and I had parted.

'But, Yaff, it's us together.' Her eyes shone. 'I can't do it without you. I need your strength. And love and—'

She tailed away... 'What? You don't want to stay with me? I can't do this alone. I depend on you.'

I had no idea. Shocked. Yes, I thought the universe of her, but *this?* 'Le-an, I...' Worlds of opportunity and fulfilment were opening up in my mind – worlds closed for so long. Not reluctant. Just not having realised.

She was there, at the Big Event, Upea. Performing and displaying, for a concerta and exhibition. The main attraction for the whole event. Afterwards, there was a personal meet-the-Great Upea occasion, and the queues were long. Longer than for Lele-Anna, of course, and everyone else put together. But not as long as they used to be, as I recalled.

Anyway, Lele-Anna had never had any queue for her service before, 'I've had to commence a booking system for the salon,' she said. 'It's all your credit – your support and... and everything.'

By accident, entirely so, I glimpsed *Her* as she stood and chattered, selfied, smiled and signed. That same iridescence of malachite. Or perhaps not the most gleaming I'd ever seen – but who can forever go from height to ever-greater height?

The vivvy coverage was extensive, of course – Upea, the great star, at her magnificent peak. I watched without feeling.

'Or not her peak any longer,' one critic royale said. 'This isn't her best.'

'It hasn't been her finest for the last four concerta and showings,' said another.

'Her first non-sell-out in years,' claimed another source.

'Her star is on the wane.'

We left it alone, Le-an and I. Made love as we hadn't before. Okoi, she began it, and ran with it. I flew with her, like tangled kites on high. And below us, I saw Upea.

ABOUT THE AUTHOR

Trevor is a Nottinghamshire, UK writer. His short stories and poems have frequently won prizes, and he has appeared on television discussing local matters.

As well as short stories – Sci-fi and otherwise – he has published many reader-friendly books and articles, mostly about volcanoes around the world, and dinosaur footprints on Yorkshire's Jurassic coast.

He spent fourteen years at the classroom chalkface; sixteen as headteacher of a special school; and sixteen as an Ofsted school inspector to round it off. His teacher wife now jokes that it's "Sleeping with the Enemy".

In the 1980s, his Ph.D. research pioneered the use of computers in the education of children with profound learning difficulties.

Log on to the author's website at https://www.sci-fi-author.com/
Or the dedicated Amazon site https://www.amazon.co.uk/Trevor-Watts/e/B085GLPLKQ%3Fref=dbs_a_mng_rwt_scns_share

Facebook @ Creative Imagination
  https://www.facebook.com/Creative-Imagination-101803121373802/?modal=admin_todo_tour
And
https://www.facebook.com/graham.watts.545

BY THE SAME AUTHOR

OF OTHER TIMES AND SPACES

The Giant Anthology – 460 pages with 39 tales of here and now, and the futures that await us.

If you were spying on another planet, would you do any better than Dicky and Miriam in the snappy two-pager "Air Sacs and Frilly Bits".

Could you live among the laughs and lovers of "I'm a Squumaid"? Or cope with the heartache of "The Twelve Days of Crystal-Ammas"?

In the novella-length "The Colonist", how could anyone fault Davvy's actions in setting up Hill Six-Four-Six with a party of Highraff refugee women and children?

How might you cope in class with the all-knowing "Thank you, Mellissa" and her little yellow ducks?

AMAZON 5* READER REVIEWS
- "Sci-fi at its most original"
- "Absolutely excellent, equal with anything I have read in the genre, including all the old masters when I was a kid."
- "Great entertainment and good stories from start to finish."
- "A sci-fi feast – I highly recommend it."

The New-Classic Sci-Fi Series

Details of contents of all books are on Trevor's website at www.sci-fi-author.com. Exact details of timing for the release of later books will find their way there as soon as they are known. Hopeful speculation about the target dates litters the blog you can find there.

Zero 9-4 Book 1 in the New-Classic Series of Sci-Fi from the Lighter Side.

AMAZON 5* READER REVIEWS
"Loved the sheer variety on offer."
"A great book of short stories to delight any sci-fi reader's palette."
"Go on, give yourself a treat."
"More than 20 stories – loved every one."

Does Cleanup foretell the future of humanity? Or is it in the hands of the scientists who believe the key to space-time manipulation is Zero 9-4? Or is They Call the Wind Pariah a premonition of our fate in the grip of the Corona virus?

Are the aliens already among us in Betty? Or in the fire pit of Kalai Alaa?

Dare you immerse yourself in the laughs and trials to come in It isn't easy Being a Hero, or Holes aren't my Thing.

Are you prepared to join the war of the alien genders in Kjid, or Typical Man?

ORBITAL SPAM

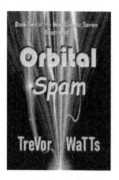

Book 2 in the New-Classic Series of Sci-Fi from the Lighter Side.
AMAZON READER REVIEWS
"A great selection"
"A heads up on this third one I've read by this author"
"My kind of real characters – I get their humour and dilemmas and problems and solutions – or failures, sometimes."

What would you do if you suspect your ship's been dumped in the Orbital Spam folder?

Is there anything you can you do when the Great Pondkeeper up in the sky decides to call time? Or when a trail of disembodied footprints heads straight for you across the wet concrete in Self-Levelling, how do you respond?

Would you answer the Prasap1 call?

These 20+ tales will alter your view of the future. The illustrations will brighten a boring wait at the space-port, or leisurely evening in orbit. Plus one poem: the beautiful, mysterious and stranded child – Mirador.

In his welcoming speech at the Xaatan Peace Conference, the Galactic High Commissioner described this book as, "The most entertaining read I've had in seven millennia... a great step forward for humanity."

TERMINAL SPACE

Book 3 in the New-Classic Series.
READER REVIEWS

"5* because it's basically the best sci-fi I've read for years."

"Surprised I was so taken up with these stories – Excellent."

"Completely absorbed in some of these situations – the atmosphere and the so-believable characters."

Twenty+ terrific Sci-Fi stories from the here and now and maybe-then, with illustrations.

➢ When Prisoner 296 is sent to carry out repairs in the Khuk spaceport's entrance tunnel at rush hour, will he find out why it's known as The Terminal Space?

➢ What on Earth can the alien do when he's stuck in traffic and going to miss his spaceship home?

➢ Could it be you who writes the heartfelt plea to Agony Aunt, Maar'juh'rih?

➢ If it depended on you, would there Always be an England?

➢ When it comes to that vital First Contact moment, would your first message be the same as the one that Polly settled on?

As Princess Porkyu said at the Cygnus Arms in 2929, "Laugh or catch your breath; shed a tear or cheer them on, you'll immerse yourself with these souls of the universe."

Twists & Turns

Book 1 in the Series of Short Stories from the Odds, Sods and Surprises side of life.

READER REVIEWS
"Superb stories."
"Such different situations, characters and moods."
"Very, very readable…"
"This book lifted my spirit."
"Compelling gems – whether light, funny or sombre, they are all rewarding and totally absorbing."
"There's nothing routine here."

"41 Terrific Stories"

Do you think you could live up to a Category Four Name?
Baksheesh Bill could save the life of the enemy fighter pilot, but will he?
Quiz Night is all about questions, but what's going to be her answer to the last one?
The *Prim* Reaper? Who are you kidding?
It's the most expensive thing in the place – Please! Not my Mirror!
Something about her caught my instant attention, and it wasn't only the Three Silver Buttons.

BOOKS TO COME

Roads Less Travelled

The second collection in the odds, sods & surprises series of short stories from the Silver Side. (OsssOssss2).

You think *you've* had problems with your satnav?

What's on the menu tonight at the Truckers' Brass Kettle Diner?

Igor, the traffic warden, will not be moved..

Is there something promising, or threatening, about the woman in the car in the other lane?

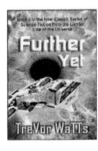

Book 5 in the New-Classic Sci-Fi Series.

Under interrogation, would you give them the secret of Vondur'Eye, regardless of the consequences?

What comes shimmering along the beach?

Effo the maths genius has forgotten... what?

Your colony ship's suffered a breach – Level 1. So where does your future lie now?

Worlds of Wonder
Book of Poetry

Collected poems that everyone
Can see themselves reflected in.
Of flower-strewn girls, of ponies gone,
A ranch-hand wreaks the deadly sin.

Filling up the parting glass;
Of cats and men and ladies, too.
World War One and graves en masse;
Of dynamite and the Devil's brew.

Machu Picchu and Galway Town
Whoever said Old men don't fall?
From Java's mud to nature's gown
The pages here unveil them all

Minimum arrestable delinquency;
The haggis that truly took my heart;
In elegant idiosyncrasy
I take my leave, I must depart.

Taking it Personally
OsssOssss3

Thirty-five short stories about the
  things that people do.
What The Boss said was most
  regrettable, but he has to live with
  it.
Would Uncle Dave allow the thieving
  creature into his cardboard castle?
You think you're in the cells for a
  night? Think again.